Kate Freiligrath-Kroeker, Mary Sibree

Alice and other fairy plays for children

Kate Freiligrath-Kroeker, Mary Sibree

Alice and other fairy plays for children

ISBN/EAN: 9783337214647

Printed in Europe, USA, Canada, Australia, Japan

Cover: Foto ©Andreas Hilbeck / pixelio.de

More available books at **www.hansebooks.com**

ALICE

AND

Other Fairy Plays for Children.

BY

KATE FREILIGRATH-KROEKER.

WITH

EIGHT ORIGINAL PLATES AND FOUR PICTURE-INITIALS,

BY

MARY SIBREE.

WITH ORIGINAL AND ADAPTED MUSIC.

LONDON:

GEORGE BELL AND SONS, YORK STREET,

COVENT GARDEN.

1881.

CONTENTS.

PREFACE.

LIKE most plays of this kind, these fairy dramas were originally written to supply a " home demand." They are now presented to the public in a collective form, a dramatic version of Mr. Lewis Carroll's " Alice " being added to the original plays.

I have to express my sincerest gratitude to Mr. Lewis Carroll for the permission to dramatise his charming story, which he most courteously granted to me. Wherever the dramatic exigences demanded inevitable alterations or additions, I earnestly hope these have been executed in the true fairy spirit of the original.

I have also much pleasure in thanking Miss K. Field for her kind permission to make use of the music, expressly composed by her for " Snowdrop," on the occasion of its being performed, two years ago, at the Hackney High School.

In conclusion, I have only to express my earnest desire that my little volume may gain friends everywhere among children, for whom it was written.

FOREST HILL, KENT.
  October, 1879.

ALICE.

B

INCIDENTAL REMARKS TO " ALICE."

THE costumes and masks of the different characters in
" Alice " should be copied as faithfully as possible from
Mr. Tenniel's illustrations to " Alice in Wonderland,"
as well as from those to " Through the Looking-Glass."
A few words may be necessary as to the representation
of the " Cheshire Cat," which can be easily managed,
though at first sight seemingly difficult. The *head* of
the Cat should be drawn and painted on cardboard, and
afterwards cut out. It must be exactly like the original,
only in *enlarged size*, so as to be distinctly visible to the
audience. The head must be suspended from a line
drawn across the stage, and should be able to be drawn
up or down, at pleasure, from the sides. When Alice first
sees the *grin* of the Cat, only the mouth of the animal
should be visible ; the rest of the head being enveloped
by a *cosy of grey gauze*. This must be gently raised,
as the Cat gradually gets in his features, until it is
finally quite withdrawn, leaving the head free. The Cat

must be suspended two or three feet above Alice's head,
in centre of stage, and must be perfectly visible to the
audience.   Of course the raising of the gauze cosy
must be practised beforehand, that there may be no
hitch at the time of the performance.

Dramatis Personæ.

ALICE.
QUEEN OF HEARTS.
* KING OF HEARTS.
THE DUCHESS.
* HER COOK.
* THE WHITE QUEEN.
THE CHESHIRE CAT.
THE EXECUTIONER.
THE HATTER.
THE MARCH HARE.
* THE DORMOUSE.
THE WALRUS.
THE CARPENTER.
THE LION.
THE UNICORN.
* THE GRYPHON. } These two do not appear on the stage
* THE MOCK TURTLE.} at all, but are only heard.
* A FISH FOOTMAN.
* TWO OF SPADES. }
* FIVE OF SPADES. } Gardeners to Queen.
* SEVEN OF SPADES. }

---

* The *rôles* marked by an asterisk are so slight that the children acting them can easily take two of the parts so distinguished, thus reducing the number of actors considerably, if necessary.

ALICE.

ACT I.—GOING TO THE QUEEN'S CROQUET PARTY.

Scene—*A Garden.*

SCENE I.

Enter three gardeners (SPADES) and walk up to a large standard rose-tree, which is full of white roses. They begin to paint them red. Enter ALICE, who watches them curiously.

TWO OF SPADES.

LOOK out now, Five! Don't go splashing paint over me like that!

FIVE OF SPADES (*sulkily*).

I couldn't help it. Seven jogged my elbow.

SEVEN OF SPADES.

That's right, Five! Always lay the blame on others!

FIVE.

You 'd better not talk! I heard the Queen say only yesterday, you deserved to be beheaded!

TWO.

What for?

SEVEN.

That's none of your business, Two.

FIVE.

Yes, it *is* his business—and I'll tell him—it was for bringing the cook tulip-roots instead of onions.

SEVEN (*throwing down his brush*).

Well—of all unjust things (*sees* ALICE, *and suddenly stops. The others look round also, and all of them bow low*).

ALICE (*timidly*).

Would you tell me, please, why you are painting those roses?

(FIVE AND SEVEN *say* *nothing, and look at* TWO).

TWO (*after slight pause in a low tone*).

Why, the fact is, you see, Miss, this here ought to have been a *red* rose-tree, and we put a white one in by mistake; and if the Queen was to find it out, we should all have our heads cut off, you know. So you see, Miss, we're doing our best afore she comes to——

FIVE (*who has been looking anxiously across the garden*).

The Queen! the Queen!

TWO, FIVE, AND SEVEN (*instantly throw themselves flat on their faces round the rose-tree*).

ALICE (*looking round eagerly*).

Yes, there they come. What a number of people! I wonder whether *I* ought to throw myself on my face, like the three gardeners! I can't remember if there is such a rule at Processions. And besides, what would be the use of a Procession if people had all to lie down on their faces, so that they couldn't see it! No, I'll stand here and wait!

Enter QUEEN OF HEARTS, KING OF HEARTS, *and* EXECUTIONER.

QUEEN (*shouting and waving her hand*).

Go back!   Go back!   You're *not* to come this way.

(*Tramp of feet is heard behind scene as of many people passing, also beat of drum and fife, and blasts of trumpet.*)

QUEEN (*seeing* ALICE).

Who are you?   What's your name, child?

ALICE (*politely, somewhat tremulously*).

My name is Alice, so please your Majesty.   (*Aside*) Why, they're only a pack of cards after all.   I needn't be afraid of them!

QUEEN.

And what do you want here?

ALICE.

I wanted to see the Procession.

QUEEN.

There *is* no Procession.   At least not here.   The Procession has gone round by the back way.

ALICE.

May I ask why, your Majesty?

QUEEN.

Yes, you may *ask*. (*Looks into air vacantly.*)

ALICE (*waiting for answer*).

May I ask why, your Majesty?

QUEEN.

Certainly, you may ask!

ALICE.

Then why does the Procession go the other way?

QUEEN.

Oh, you want an answer too? Why didn't you say so? I thought you only wanted to *ask*. Well, I don't mind telling *you*, but you mustn't tell any one else! Promise? or your head will go off! You see I never go out without my Executioner! I don't know what I should do without him, he's *so* useful!—Well, do you promise?

ALICE (*smiling*).

Yes, I promise.

QUEEN.

Then I'll tell you! The Procession goes round behind the scenes, because we haven't enough people for it.

ALICE.

Haven't enough people?

QUEEN.

Don't you understand? How stupid you are! You can't have Processions without people—can you, now?

ALICE.

No, certainly not! At least, I don't think so.

QUEEN.

Well, then, we haven't enough people for the Procession; because we want ten soldiers, ten courtiers, ten royal children. Then come all the guests, and we *never* have less than ten, and often twenty,—that makes forty, you see; then there are the kings and queens, white rabbits, and all the other animals to swell the ranks. Now, if they go the back way, no one sees if there are four or forty, whereas, if they passed by here, a Procession of four people *would* look ridiculous, wouldn't it?

ALICE.

Oh, I see!

QUEEN.

Yes, that's the reason. But the King and the Executioner always accompany me wherever I go—— (*seeing gardeners, who are still lying on their faces round rose-tree*)—and who are *these?*

ALICE.

How should *I* know? It's no business of *mine!*

QUEEN (*glares at her and screams*).

Off with her head! Off with her head!

ALICE.

Nonsense! Don't talk rubbish!

KING (*timidly to* QUEEN).

Consider, my dear. She is only a child!

QUEEN.

Turn them over! (*pointing to gardeners*).

KING *carefully turns them over one by one with his foot.*

TWO.
FIVE.
SEVEN.
} *Jump up and bow to* KING, QUEEN, *and* ALICE, *without stopping.*

QUEEN.

Leave off that! You make me giddy. (*Looks at rose-tree.*) What *have* you been doing here?

TWO (*going down on one knee, humbly*).

May it please your Majesty, we were trying——

QUEEN.

I see! Off with their heads! (*goes on.*)

(THREE GARDENERS *run behind* ALICE *for protection.*)

ALICE.

You *shan't* be beheaded!

QUEEN (*shouting and going off the stage*).

Are their heads off?

EXECUTIONER (*shouting*).

Their heads are gone, if it please your Majesty!

QUEEN (*nearly off stage, still shouting*).

Can you play croquet, Alice?

ALICE (*shouting*).

Yes!

QUEEN (*roaring*).

Come on, then! I invite you to my croquet party!

[*Exeunt* QUEEN, KING, *and* EXECUTIONER.

Scene II.

ALICE.

Oh, dear, I don't think I'll follow her—at least, not yet! She's sure to want to cut my head off! What a temper she has, to be sure!

Enter the Duchess *and her* Cook.

(Cook *carries the baby, which she dredges with pepper from a pepper-castor.*)

Ah! I've met *her* before! Where was it? I forget, I've been in so many queer places to-day, and have seen so many strange things. Oh, I know, it was in the Duchess's kitchen! (*sneezing.*) Goodness gracious, what a lot of pepper!

DUCHESS (*sneezing*).

If everybody minded their own business, the world would go round a deal faster than it does. And the moral of that is——

ALICE.

Do you think that would be an advantage, Duchess?

pepper then, little dear! (*Tosses baby up and down, singing*):

"I speak severely to my boy,
    I beat him, when he sneezes,
For he can thoroughly enjoy
    The pepper when he pleases!"

BABY.

Wow! wow! wow!

DUCHESS (*throwing baby to* COOK).

Here, take the child! I'm off now—can't be wasting all the afternoon like this. Dredge the baby well, if it cries, with pepper. He'll soon stop crying then!

COOK.

But I can't nurse the baby and make the soup too!

DUCHESS (*stamping her foot*).

You can!

COOK.

I can't!

DUCHESS.

You shall!

COOK.

I shan't!

ALICE.

Gracious! they're beginning all over again!

DUCHESS (*to* ALICE).

Will *you* mind the baby?

ALICE.

Well—I'm afraid I can't manage it properly, you see!

DUCHESS.

Well, will you come and play croquet? *Do,* there's a dear old thing!

ALICE.

I will presently, but not now. (*Aside*) I'm not a dear *old* thing, anyhow, and I don't want to play with *her!*

DUCHESS (*offended*).

As you please! I'm off.

COOK (*screaming after her*).

Here, you take the baby!

DUCHESS (*screaming back*).

I shan't!

COOK (*throwing the pepper-dredge after her*).
Then you take *that!*

DUCHESS.

Thank you.   It didn't hit me!   [*Exit.*

COOK (*throwing baby after her*).
Then take that, too!   I'm off to look after my soup.
[*Exit the other side, sulkily.*

DUCHESS (*reappearing and throwing baby after* COOK).
I tell you, I will *not* take the child!   [*Exit quickly.*

ALICE (*looking dismayed after both*).
Well, I never!   Throwing babies about like *that!*
I wonder if they like it, poor little things!   What
next?

SCENE III.

Enter WHITE QUEEN, *running hard.* *She stops when she sees* ALICE. FISH FOOTMAN *appears.*

WHITE QUEEN (*wringing her hands*).

Bread-and-butter! oh, bread-and-butter!

FISH FOOTMAN.

I beg your pardon, ma'am; but my orders are, you must not come in here.

WHITE QUEEN.

Why not? oh, please, why not?

FISH FOOTMAN.

Because here is the boundary line. You come from Looking-Glass Land, and this is Wonderland! Well, it stands to reason you can't be running about *both*, you know.

WHITE QUEEN (*piteously, pointing to* ALICE).

But look at *her!* She's been in Looking-Glass

Land, and she's in Wonderland! If *she* can, why can't *I?*

FISH FOOTMAN.

I don't know why, but them's my orders. What would be the result, I should like to know, if all the people of Looking-Glass Land were to get mixed up with the people of Wonderland?

ALICE.

I think it would be great fun!

FISH FOOTMAN (*shaking his head solemnly*).

Ah, but you haven't got to keep order, you see! That makes all the difference.

WHITE QUEEN.

Oh dear, oh dear! Bread-and-butter! Bread-and-butter!

ALICE.

Am I addressing the White Queen?

WHITE QUEEN.

Well, yes, if you call that a dressing. It isn't *my* notion of the thing at all.

ALICE (*aside*).

She's dreadfully untidy, poor thing! Every single

thing's crooked! And she's all over pins! (*Aloud*) May I put your shawl right for you?

WHITE QUEEN.

I don't know what's the matter with it. It's out of temper, I think. I've pinned it here and I've pinned it there, but there's no pleasing it!

ALICE.

It *can't* go straight, you know, if you pin it all on one side. And oh, dear me, what a state your hair is in!

WHITE QUEEN (*sighing*).

The brush has got entangled in it. And I lost the comb yesterday.

ALICE (*arranging her hair*).

Come, you look rather better now. But, really, you should have a lady's maid.

WHITE QUEEN.

I'm sure I'll take you with pleasure. Twopence a week and jam every other day!

ALICE (*laughing*).

I don't want you to hire *me*. And I don't care for jam.

WHITE QUEEN.

It's very good jam.

ALICE.

Well, I don't want it to-day, at any rate.

WHITE QUEEN.

You couldn't have it, if you did. The rule is, jam *to-morrow*, and jam *yesterday*—but *never* jam *to-day!*

ALICE.

But it must come *sometimes* jam to-day!

WHITE QUEEN.

No, it can't. It's jam every *other* day. To-day isn't any other day, you know.

ALICE.

I don't understand you. It's dreadfully confusing.

WHITE QUEEN.

That's the effect of living backwards, it always makes one a little giddy at first.

ALICE.

Living backwards! I never heard of such a thing!

Enter FISH FOOTMAN.

If you please, Miss Alice, the Queen says that if you don't come to play croquet with her, in double quick time, she'll have your head off.

WHITE QUEEN.

Croquet! Going to play at croquet! Oh, I wish I were going to play croquet too! One gets so tired of always playing chess, you know.

ALICE.

I don't want to go. *You* go instead. (*To* FISH FOOTMAN) I pass this lady on to the Queen's croquet ground. So let her in, please. She's a White Queen, although she *is* rather untidy! You can say I am coming by-and-by.

FISH FOOTMAN.

Well, if her head's chopped off, don't put the blame on *me*, that's all!

WHITE QUEEN.

Oh, thank you so much! I wish you would come and be my lady's maid, dear! Twopence a week, and jam every other day, you know!

[*Exeunt* WHITE QUEEN *and* FISH FOOTMAN.

ALICE.

Yes, so you said before! (*Calling after her*) Take care, your shawl is coming off again, and I see two hair-pins sticking out. Dear, dear, how untidy she is, poor thing! I think I'll go home again; I do *not* want to go to the Queen's croquet party; and, what's more, I don't mean to go, unless she comes to fetch me herself, and then I suppose I *must!* Heigho! Why, what is that? (*Looks up and sees the grin of the* CHESHIRE CAT *suspended in the air in the middle of the stage.**) It's a grin—no, it isn't—yes, it is—why, it's the Cheshire Cat I saw in the Duchess's kitchen! This *is* nice! Now I shall have somebody to talk to.

CAT (*gradually getting more features in*).

How are you getting on?

ALICE (*aside*).

I must wait till the eyes appear—oh, here they are! It's no use speaking to it, though, till its ears have come, or at least *one* of them.

CAT (*whose head now appears fully*).

There, that's all you will see of me just now. That's quite enough for to-day. Now, *how* are you getting on at the croquet party?

---

* *See* Incidental Remarks, pp. 3 and 4.

ALICE.

Well, I haven't been there yet, and, to tell you the truth, I don't much care to go. The Queen quarrels so dreadfully with everybody, that I am quite afraid of her.

CAT.

How do you like the Queen?

ALICE.

Not at all! She's so extremely——

Enter KING *hurriedly.*

KING (*not seeing head of* CHESHIRE CAT *in air*).

Who *are* you talking to, pray? And why don't you come to play croquet with the Queen? She'll be so angry, she'll have your head off if she finds you here. (*Seeing* CAT) What *is* that you are talking to?

ALICE.

It's a friend of mine—a Cheshire Cat. Allow me to introduce it.

KING.

I don't like the look of it at all. However, it may kiss my hand if it likes.

CAT.

I'd rather not.

KING (*getting behind* ALICE).

Don't be impertinent—and don't look at me like that.

ALICE.

A cat may look at a king. I've read that in some book, but I don't remember where.

KING.

Well, it must be removed, that's all I know! (*Enter* QUEEN.) My dear, I wish you would have this Cat removed. I don't like it.

QUEEN.

Off with his head!

KING.

I thought you would say so. I'll go and fetch the Executioner myself. [*Exit* KING.

ALICE (*to* CAT).

I say, don't you think you had better go home? Even the pepper in the Duchess's kitchen is better than this.

CAT.

No, I don't mind. I'll stay where I am, I think.
Thank you all the same, though.

QUEEN.

What a long time they are coming!

Enter KING *and* EXECUTIONER.

KING.

I've run so hard, I'm quite out of breath. Here he
is, my dear, here he is! Pray, repeat your commands!

QUEEN (*pointing to* CAT'S *head*).

Off with his head!

EXECUTIONER.

Where *is* he? I don't see him! In fact, I can't
see anybody.

QUEEN.

Don't you see the Cat, you stupid man?

KING.

Can't you see him up there, grinning as large as
life?

ALICE (*aside*).

Poor Cheshire Cat! It's all over with him, I'm afraid!

EXECUTIONER (*seeing* CAT).

Him!

CAT (*benignly*).

Yes, old fellow, they mean *me*. Look hard at me, while you're about it!

KING.

Yes, that Cat!

QUEEN.

Don't you understand English?

EXECUTIONER.

Yes, I do! What then?

QUEEN.

You're to chop his head off!

EXECUTIONER.

I can't!

QUEEN.

You can't?

KING (*faintly*).

He can't!

CAT (*quietly*).

I thought as much.

EXECUTIONER.

No, I can't. And, what's more, I won't, that's flat.
A likely idea that!

KING.

What do you mean ?

QUEEN.

How dare you ?

ALICE (*aside*).

Oh, I *am* so glad !

EXECUTIONER.

I mean what I say. I can't. And I'll tell you
why. This is my argument. You can't cut off a
head unless there's a body to cut it from. That's
nature, that is. You *cannot* cut a head off, unless
there's a body to cut it from. I've never had such a
thing to do before, and I'm not going to begin at *my*
time of life.

KING.

Well, that may be *your* argument. And a very poor
one it is, to my idea. Now you look here—this is *my*
argument—everything that's got a head can be beheaded.
So don't talk nonsense, and do your duty.

QUEEN.

Argument, indeed ! Fiddlesticks ! If something

isn't done about this preposterous business in less than no time, I'll have everybody executed all round!   And that's *my* argument!

ALICE.

Please your Majesty, the Cat belongs to the Duchess, hadn't you better ask her about it?

QUEEN (*to* EXECUTIONER).

Go and fetch her here directly!

Enter DUCHESS, *running.*

DUCHESS.

Oh, I hope I'm not too late for the game; for the moral of that would be—— (*suddenly sees* QUEEN *and stops, then says faintly*)—A fine day, your Majesty!

QUEEN.

A fine day!   A fine—— oh, cut off her head!   Cut off her head, and be quick about it!   Why do you allow your cats to go about to Queen's croquet parties, insulting people?   Do you know you can be beheaded for that?

DUCHESS (*very faintly*).

Cat, your Majesty?   *Where,* your Majesty?

[CAT *vanishes.*

QUEEN (*pointing upwards*).

Yes, Cat!—look at the vicious brute grinning away—— Why, where is he gone?

KING (*running up and down*).

Oh, the Cat! The Cat! Where is the Cat?

EXECUTIONER (*sulkily*).

Well, as I suppose you don't go so far as to want me to behead something that does not exist, I think I'll go home! [*Exit.*

QUEEN (*affectionately to* ALICE).

And now, after our *very* pleasant afternoon, let us go on with our croquet! You don't know how nice it is—the mallets are real flamingoes, and the arches are soldiers doubled up, and the balls are live hedgehogs!

ALICE.

What a very funny game!

QUEEN.

Ah, I thought you would like it! Come along! (*To* DUCHESS) You may come too, if you like!

D

DUCHESS.

Oh, thank you, your Majesty!

KING.

You are pardoned, you know!

ALICE (*going off arm-in-arm with the* QUEEN).

Come, *that*'s a good thing! Now for croquet! What next, I wonder?

[*Exeunt* ALICE, KING, *and* QUEEN.

CURTAIN.

ACT II.—THE HATTER'S TEA-PARTY.

SCENE.—*A large table is set out in a garden under a tree. Cups and saucers are laid all round. Arm-chair at top of table. Chairs all round it.* THE HATTER *and the* MARCH HARE *are discovered sitting at the upper end of table, facing the audience. The* DORMOUSE *is sitting between them, fast asleep. They are resting their elbows on it, as if it were a cushion.*

Enter ALICE.

ALICE.

I'm so glad I escaped from the croquet lawn! (*Seeing the tea-party*) Dear me! How very uncomfortable for the Dormouse, to be sure! but, as he is asleep, I suppose he doesn't mind.

HATTER (*seeing* ALICE).

No room! No room!

MARCH HARE (*waving his teacup*).

No room! No room!

ALICE (*indignantly sitting down in arm-chair*).

There is *plenty* of room! How can you say so?

MARCH HARE (*politely*).

Have some wine?

ALICE (*looking all round table*).

I don't see any wine.

MARCH HARE.

You're quite right. There *isn't* any.

ALICE (*angrily*).

Then it wasn't very civil of you to offer it.

MARCH HARE.

It wasn't very civil of you to sit down without being invited.

ALICE (*aside*).

Dear me, how all these creatures *will* argue! (*Aloud*) I didn't know it was *your* table. It's laid for a great many more than three.

HATTER (*looking hard at* ALICE).

Your hair wants cutting.

ALICE.

You should learn not to make personal remarks. It's very rude.

HATTER.

Oh, is it ? Why is a raven like a writing-desk ?

ALICE (*aside*).

Come, we shall have some fun now. I'm glad they've begun asking riddles, it's so much better than arguing. (*Aloud*) I believe I can guess that.

MARCH HARE.

Do you mean that you think you can find out the answer to it?

ALICE.

Exactly so.

MARCH HARE.

Then you should say what you mean.

ALICE.

I do. At least—at least, I mean what I say—that's the same thing, you know !

HATTER.

Not the same thing a bit. Why, you might just as

well say that " I see what I eat " is the same thing as
" I eat what I see ! "

MARCH HARE.

You might just as well say that " I like what I get "
is the same thing as " I get what I like."

DORMOUSE (*without looking up*).

You might just as well say that " I breathe when I
sleep " is the same as " I sleep when I breathe."

HATTER.

It *is* the same thing with *you!* (*To* ALICE) Have
you guessed the riddle yet?

ALICE.

No ; I give it up. What's the answer ?

HATTER.

I haven't the slightest idea.

MARCH HARE.

Nor I.

ALICE (*sighing*).

I really think you might do something better with the
time than wasting it in riddles that have no answers !

HATTER.

If you knew Time as well as I do, you wouldn't talk about wasting *it*. It's *him*.

ALICE.

I don't know what you mean!

HATTER (*contemptuously*).

Of course you don't! I dare say you never even spoke to Time.

ALICE (*cautiously*).

Perhaps not—but I know I have to beat time when I learn music.

HATTER.

Ah, that accounts for it. He won't stand beating. Now, if you only kept on good terms with him, he'd do almost anything you liked with the clock. For instance, suppose it were nine in the morning, just time to begin lessons, you'd only have to whisper a hint to Time, and round goes the clock in a twinkling. Half-past one, time for dinner!

MARCH HARE.

I only wish it was.

ALICE.

That would be grand, certainly; but then—I shouldn't perhaps be hungry for it, you know.

HATTER.

Not at first, perhaps.   But you could keep it to half-past one as long as you liked.

ALICE.

Is that the way you manage ?

HATTER *(mournfully shaking his head).*

Not I !   We quarrelled last March—just before he went mad, you know *(pointing with his teaspoon at the* MARCH HARE, *who sighs too).*   It was at the great concert given by the Queen of Hearts, I remember.   And I had to sing :

> " Twinkle, twinkle, little bat,
>   How I wonder what you're at——"

You know the song, perhaps ?

ALICE.

I've heard something like it.

HATTER.

It goes on, you know, in this way:

> " Up above the world you fly,
>   Like a tea-tray in the sky :
>   Twinkle, twinkle, little——"

DORMOUSE (*shakes himself, and goes on singing in his sleep*).

" Twinkle, twinkle, twinkle, twinkle——"

HATTER (*indignantly*).

Stop that, I say !

DORMOUSE (*without taking any notice, goes on singing*).

" Twinkle, twinkle, twinkle——"

MARCH HARE (*angrily*).

Don't you hear ? You're not to make that noise !

DORMOUSE (*as before*).

" Twinkle, twinkle, twinkle, twinkle, twinkle——"

HATTER.

Pinch him, please, March Hare !

MARCH HARE.

Pinch him, please, brother ! (*They pinch him.*)

DORMOUSE (*waking up*).

Oh, I say ! you're pinching me ! What's that for ?

HATTER.

You stop twinkling, then !

MARCH HARE.

Or we'll do it again !

(DORMOUSE *falls asleep again between them.*)

HATTER (*to* ALICE).

Well, I had hardly finished the first verse, when the Queen bawled out, " Off with his head!   He's murdering the time ! "

ALICE.

How dreadfully savage !

HATTER (*mournfully*).

And ever since that he won't do a thing I ask.   It's always six o'clock now !

ALICE.

Oh ! is *that* the reason so many tea-things are put out here ?

HATTER (*sighing*).

Yes, that's it.   It's always tea-time, and we've no time to wash the things between whiles.

ALICE.

Then you keep moving round, I suppose ?

HATTER.

Exactly so—as the things get used up.

ALICE.

But what happens when you come to the beginning again ?

MARCH HARE (*yawning*).

Suppose we change the subject ! I'm getting tired of this cup. Let's all move one place down.

ALICE.

But then I'll get a dirty one !

HATTER.

Never mind ! (*Moves down one chair.*)

MARCH HARE *moves down one chair.*

DORMOUSE, *fast asleep, moves down one chair.*

ALICE *moves down one chair.*

Enter FISH FOOTMAN.

FISH FOOTMAN (*to* HATTER).

If you please, sir, there's the Walrus and the Carpenter outside, and they want to know whether they may come in to tea.

HATTER.

Certainly *not.*

MARCH HARE.

We don't want them.

ALICE.

Oh, please, *do* let them come! I should like to see them so much!

HATTER (*offended*).

Are we not enough company, pray?

MARCH HARE.

Or good enough for *you*, I should like to know? There—(*to* FISH FOOTMAN) tell them we don't want them; but they may come in, if they like!

[*Exit* FISH FOOTMAN.

Enter the WALRUS *and the* CARPENTER, *arm-in-arm.*

WALRUS (*solemnly lifting up his right hand*).

" The time has come, the Walrus said "—
That's *myself*, you know.

CARPENTER.

Of course we know *that*. *I* 'm not a walrus, I believe !

WALRUS.

Who said you were?   Don't interrupt, brother.   As
I was saying :

" The time has come, the Walrus said,
    To talk of many things ;
Of shoes, of ships, and sealing-wax,
    And cabbages, and kings ;
And why the tea is boiling hot ;
    And whether pigs have wings ! "

CARPENTER (*looking all over table, growling*).

I don't see any oysters here, Walrus !

WALRUS.

What a shame !   After we have come so far, too,
and trotted so quick !

ALICE.

Do people eat oysters for tea? I didn't know that! This is a *tea*-party, you know, not an oyster-party.

HATTER (*pointing with his teaspoon to empty chair next to his*).

Never mind about oysters! Sit down there.

WALRUS (*sitting down*).

But I *do* mind! No oysters, brother!

CARPENTER (*sitting down next to* WALRUS).

Cut us another slice!

WALRUS.

What did you say, old man?

CARPENTER (*crossly*).

Cut us another slice. I wish you were not quite so deaf; I've had to ask you twice!

ALICE,

Dear me! They are not such good company as I thought they would be. They are so greedy!

Enter FISH FOOTMAN.

FISH FOOTMAN.

Please, sir, here's somebody else, now, wanting to come in.

HATTER.

Who is it?

FISH FOOTMAN.

The Lion and the Unicorn, if you please, sir.

MARCH HARE.

Then move down another place.

(ALL *get up and move down one place.*)

HATTER.

Have they got a plum-cake?

FISH FOOTMAN.

The Lion is carrying one, I believe, sir. Leastways, it smelt like plum-cake, sir.

MARCH HARE.

Then let them come in!

CARPENTER (*growling*).

Plum-cake! I don't want no plum-cake, I don't!

WALRUS (*pulling out his handkerchief*).

Plum-cake isn't oysters!

(*Dries his eyes, and then recites in broken voice:*)

"A loaf of bread, the Walrus said,"—
That's *me*, you know.

ALICE (*aside*).

He's said that before.

WALRUS.

" Is what we chiefly need ;
    Pepper and vinegar besides
    Are very good, indeed.
    Now if you're ready, oysters dear——"

(*breaking down*).

Ah, if there were only some oysters here, Carpenter!

(*weeps*).

CARPENTER (*weeping bitterly*).

Instead of which, there ain't none, Walrus dear!

ALICE.

Oh, *here* come the others! I am so glad!

Enter the LION *and the* UNICORN.

The LION *carries plum-cake, and carefully deposits
it on table. As soon as his back is turned, the*
WALRUS *and the* CARPENTER *cut it up, and begin
eating it up as fast as they can.*

UNICORN (*seeing* ALICE, *in a tone of deep disgust*).
Why—what—is—*this ?*

HATTER (*eagerly*).
This is a child !   We only found it to-day.

MARCH HARE.
It's as large as life, and twice as natural !

UNICORN.
I always thought children were fabulous monsters !
Is it alive ?

HATTER.
It can talk.

UNICORN (*dreamily*).
Then talk, child !

E

ALICE (*smiling*).

Do you know, I always thought unicorns were fabulous monsters, too? I never saw one alive before.

UNICORN.

Well, now that we *have* seen each other, if you'll believe in me, I'll believe in you. Is that a bargain?

ALICE.

Yes, if you like.

LION (*coming forward, also sees* ALICE, *and inspects her through his eyeglass*).

What's this?

UNICORN.

Ah, what *is* it, now? You'll never guess! I couldn't.

LION (*yawning*).

Are you animal—or vegetable—or mineral?

UNICORN (*triumphantly*).

It's a fabulous monster!

LION (*sitting down next to* CARPENTER).

Then hand round the plum-cake, monster!

ALICE.

Where is it gone to? Oh, it's nearly finished!
The Walrus and the Carpenter are eating it all up!

WALRUS (*speaking with his mouth full*).

It wasn't a very large cake, you see! Stupid thing
to bring such a small cake for a large tea-party!

CARPENTER.

Don't hurry, brother!

HATTER (*indignantly*).

Why, you said you didn't like plum-cake! Both
of you.

MARCH HARE.

I call that mean! Said they preferred oysters, and
finish the cake. (*To* WALRUS) So you did, you know!

WALRUS (*indifferently*).

Did I?

MARCH HARE (*as before*).

Did you? Why, of course you did!

WALRUS (*to* CARPENTER).

The night is fine, oh brother dear! Do you admire
the view?

MARCH HARE.

That's no answer!

CARPENTER.

Cut us another slice!

Enter FISH FOOTMAN.

FISH FOOTMAN.

Oh, if you please, here's another lot! They call themselves the Gryphon and the Mock Turtle. He says he's a musical gent, and he's a-sobbing fit to break his little heart. He says he wants to come to tea!

HATTER.

No, they're not to come in!

MARCH HARE.

We're quite enough as it is.

UNICORN.

There's no cake left.

LION.

There are no more teacups.

WALRUS.

Besides, they are low! They are not *real* animals, as *we* are! Gryphons and Mock Turtles! Pooh!

CARPENTER.

They don't even care for oysters, they told me one day. They said turtle soup was the only delicacy worth eating!

ALICE.

Oh, *do* let them come in, too, please! They will not do any harm.

HATTER.

Of course! *You* want everybody to come!

MARCH HARE.

You haven't got to pour out the tea.

ALICE.

But there's none poured out, as yet, by anybody, that I can see!

WALRUS.

Nor have you got to open oysters!

CARPENTER.

With a penknife too!

ALICE.

But there are no *oysters*, that I can see!

LION.

Nor have you to worry your brains with the continual baking and supplying of plum-cake!

UNICORN.

Or to stone the raisins!

ALICE.

But, really, I——

DORMOUSE (*suddenly raising his head, sings in a loud voice*).

" Twinkle, twinkle, twinkle, twinkle, twinkle, twinkle——"

HATTER (*pouring a little hot tea on its nose*).

Come, I told you not to make that noise.

DORMOUSE (*howling*).

Oh, it *is* hot!

MARCH HARE.

Of course it is! Do you think we are going to burn your nose with *cold* tea?

FISH FOOTMAN.

Then the answer is, they are *not* to come in, I suppose?

HATTER.

Certainly.

FISH FOOTMAN (*exit, and re-enters in hurry*).

Oh, if you please, they say they want to come in so badly. And the Mock Turtle, he says he'll sing a song if he may come.

MOCK TURTLE (*outside*).

Please let me come in! And I'll sing my song about the soup, you know!

HATTER.

Sing away! I'll tell you afterwards what we have decided upon.

MOCK TURTLE (*outside*).

Oh, thank you *so* much! (*singing, still outside*).

" TURTLE SOUP.

AIR.—*Beautiful Star.*

" Beautiful soup, so rich and green,
Waiting in a hot tureen!

Who for such dainties would not stoop,
Soup of the evening, beautiful soup!
Soup of the evening, beautiful soup!
   Beau-ootiful soo-oop!
   Beau-ootiful soo-oop!
Soo-oop of the e-e-evening,
   Beautiful, beautiful soup!

"Beautiful soup! Who cares for fish,
Game, or any other dish?
Who would not give all else, for twop-
ennyworth only of beautiful soup?
Pennyworth only of beautiful soup!
   Beau-ootiful soo-oop!
   Beau-ootiful soo-oop!
Soo-oop of the e-e-evening,
   Beautiful, beautiful soup!"

WALRUS (*weeping*).

That is beau-ootiful indeed! It reminds me of oysters, brother!

CARPENTER (*weeping likewise*).

So it does! So it does! It might have been oyster soup, you know! But there *are* not any, and that makes me weep, Walrus dear!

ALICE (*aside*).

They think of nothing but their oysters! Greedy things!

MOCK TURTLE (*outside, anxiously*).

May we come in, *now?*

GRYPHON (*outside*).

Please, may we come in?

HATTER (*coolly*).

I think not.

ALICE.

What! Not after that beautiful song?

DORMOUSE (*raising his head*).

" Beau-ootiful soo-oop! Beau-oo-tiful soo-oop "

MARCH HARE.

Now he's beginning again! Where's the teapot?

(DORMOUSE *falls asleep again on the table.*

MOCK TURTLE (*screaming outside*).

May we come in?

HATTER
MARCH HARE
LION
UNICORN
WALRUS
CARPENTER
} (*all shouting together*). NO!

ALICE.

Hark! What's that? What a funny noise!

(MOCK TURTLE *is heard sobbing outside very violently! Then gradually fainter by degrees, till it dies away.*)

ALICE (*after a pause*).

Poor thing! It *was* unkind of you not to let it come in!

Enter DUCHESS, *running.*

DUCHESS.

Oh, you'll catch it! You've got a tea-party, and you never invited the Queen! And she's coming straight here with the Executioner, to cut all your heads off! And the moral of that is—" Sauve qui peut !"

[*Exit running.*

WALRUS (*getting up*).

" I weep for you, the Walrus (myself) said ; I deeply sympathize——" Brother, I think we'll go home !

CARPENTER (*getting up too*).

Ah, yes, I think you're right ! A pleasant walk, a pleasant talk, upon the briny beach, you know——

WALRUS.

Just so, brother ! And we might chance to pick up an—— (*smiles*).

CARPENTER (*smiling too*).

An oyster ! Exactly.

[*Exeunt* WALRUS *and* CARPENTER.

ALICE.

Well, I'm glad *they* 're gone !

LION (*getting up and stretching himself*).

Slow tea-party, eh ? Didn't you hear a drum ?

UNICORN (*getting up*).

I think I did hear something like it in the distance ! Besides, I want to have another fight.

LION.

For the crown ?   Just so.   Good-bye, monster !

(LION *and* UNICORN *saunter out arm-in-arm.*)

ALICE.

Good-bye, Lion !   Good-bye, Unicorn !   They are at least polite, and say something ; but the other animals are dreadfully rude.

HATTER (*to* ALICE).

You had better go now.

MARCH HARE.

Or you may stay, and have your head chopped off, if you prefer it.

DORMOUSE (*raising his head*).

" To chop, chop, chop, chop, chop off last, last, last man's head ! "

ALICE.

I'm not a bit afraid !

HATTER.

Never mind.   You go home !

MARCH HARE (*waving the teapot frantically*).

Go home !   Go home !

DORMOUSE (*raising his head again*).

" There's no place like ho—ome ! "

HATTER (*angrily*).

Are you at it again ?

ALICE.

Do let me stay !

MARCH HARE.

It's too late.   Here they are !

Enter KING, QUEEN, *and* EXECUTIONER.

QUEEN (*to* ALICE).

Here's a nice state of things !   I invite you to my croquet party, and here you run away to a tea-party instead.   And at a Hatter's, too !   I wonder at you !— preferring this vulgar society to a royal croquet party ! And, pray, why wasn't *I* asked to tea ?

ALICE (*smiling*).

We didn't think you would care for such vulgar company, your Majesty.

QUEEN.

Oh, nonsense! Don't tell me! What are the simple facts of the case? You run away from my croquet party, and you go to a vulgar tea-party at a mad March Hare's and a very objectionable Hatter's; and I was never as much as asked, " Would you like a cup of tea, ma'am ? " Now, what have you to say for yourself?

ALICE.

I wanted to come here, and I didn't care for croquet. *I* can't play with live flamingoes and hedgehogs !

QUEEN (*to* KING).

Do you hear her impudence ? Off with her head !

KING (*timidly*).

But consider, my dear, she is so young——

QUEEN.

So young and so impudent ! Yes ! Now you listen to me, O King! You say another word, and *your* head will be off in a jiffey ! Executioner !

EXECUTIONER (*coming forward*).

Here I am, your Majesty !

QUEEN (*pointing to* ALICE).

Off with her head !

EXECUTIONER.

Off with her head ?   Certainly, **ma'am** !   With pleasure, ma'am !   Here is a head to cut off, you see !

ALICE.

Nonsense !   You stay where you are.

HATTER.

I told you to go home, you know.

MARCH HARE.

That's the consequence of knowing better, you see !

DORMOUSE (*singing in his sleep*).

" There's no place like ho—ome, there's no place like———"

QUEEN.

Who's that ?   (*Sees* DORMOUSE.)   Off with *his* head ! And off with *hers !*   Directly !   Do you hear ?

ALICE (*rising, and going close to footlights*).

Stuff and nonsense !   Who cares for *you*, I should

like to know? You're nothing but a——

Inside CURTAIN *falls.*

ALICE (*is left standing alone. She looks round aston-ished; when suddenly, from overhead and from every side, quantities of cards are showered upon her, so that the air is quite thick with them, and the ground is covered*).

Didn't I say so! Only a pack of cards, after all!

CURTAIN.

SPEAK ROUGHLY.

beat him when he snee-zes; He on - ly does it to an - noy, Be-
beat him when he snee-zes, For he can tho-rough-ly en - joy The

To be sung to each verse.

- cause he knows it   teases.
pep - per when he   pleases. }   Wow, wow, wow, wow,

wow, wow, wow, wow,   wow, wow, wow, wow, wow.

wow, wow, wow, wow,   wow, wow, wow, wow,   wow, wow, wow, wow, wow!

BEAUTIFUL SOUP.

SNOWDROP.

IN SEVEN SCENES.

INCIDENTAL REMARKS.

NEITHER the scenery nor the costumes in this play call for any special remark. The Seven Dwarfs should be as far as possible of the same size, so as to give an impression of uniformity. They should also be all dressed alike; brown or grey serge braided with red being very effective. Caps or hats should be made of the same material, and beards may be worn if liked. These latter, however, are not necessary.

It may here be remarked, once for all, that children, whenever they have to speak an *aside*, should be very careful *not to lower their voice in the least;* most *asides* being lost by this very common practice. Let them slightly turn their face away from the person who is not to hear the *aside,* but otherwise continue speaking as loudly as before.

Dramatis Personæ.

----◆◆----

THE QUEEN.
SNOWDROP.
PRINCE FAITHFUL.
A HUNTER.
FIRST DWARF.
SECOND DWARF.
THIRD DWARF.
FOURTH DWARF.
FIFTH DWARF.
SIXTH DWARF.
SEVENTH DWARF.

SNOWDROP.

SNOWDROP.

SCENE I.

A Room in Queen's Palace.

QUEEN.

FULL many a treasure
    lies within my
    shrine,
Pale lustrous pearls,
    and flashing dia-
    monds!
More robes of
    silky sheen
    hang in my
    rooms
Than yet I cared

to count! The richest lace
Lies scattered in profusion everywhere.
No thing so precious but I call it mine:
But still the crown of merit, Glass, is thine!

       [*Goes to the wall, and uncovers a mirror.*

Thou art my jewel, *thee* I mostly prize,
Most precious art thou, Mirror, in my eyes!
Long time it is since I consulted thee;
I'll do it now.   Let true thine answer be.

> (*Addresses the Mirror slowly.*)

"Mirror! tell me, I demand,
Who is the fairest in the land?"

> (*A faint strain of music is heard.*)

MIRROR.

"Thou the first wast wont to be,
Another fairer now than thee,
Lovely Snowdrop!—it is she!"

(QUEEN *stands amazed.   Then makes as if she
would pull down the Glass.   She stops, and
stamps her foot.*)

QUEEN.

False Glass! thou liest!   Say that once again.

> (*Silence.*)

In vain!   It never speaks but once a day!
What pangs of pain are darting through my breast!
Another fairer?   No, it shall not be!
I will destroy her, blast her beauty rare!

But soft ! she comes to-day—She'll go to-morrow !
But I will go to welcome her e'en now,
And wear the mask of friendship on my face.

[*Exit* QUEEN.

Enter PRINCE FAITHFUL, *disguised as a page.*

To-day she hath returned, my Snowdrop fair,
Unconscious that I am a mighty Prince,
Drawn hither by her beauty's potent charm.
I dare not tell her yet how much I love her,—
I dare not ask her for her own dear love.
I'll wait and see, perchance fate may befriend me.
At any rate, I'm near to her I love.
Oh ! happy hours I'll spend in waiting on her !
But here she comes, and with her comes the Queen—
A proud, fair woman; but I trust her not !
They come this way, and I will swift retire.

[*Exit* PRINCE FAITHFUL.

Enter QUEEN *and* SNOWDROP.

SNOWDROP.

I've often heard that you were beautiful,
But, dearest madam, you are fairer far
Than any people yet have told to me.

QUEEN (*aside*).

The little viper !   How she flatters me !
It shall not help her, though—the Glass spoke true !
(*Aloud*) *You* are the beauty !   How can I compare,
Old woman that I am, with your young years ?

SNOWDROP.

But, dear mamma, you're not so *very* old ;
You can't be more than thirty at the utmost ;
Considering which, you have kept wondrous well,
Scarcely a wrinkle, and not one grey hair !

QUEEN.

You do not see them, child. (*Aside*) The Glass spoke
     true ;
She is too beautiful.   She needs must die !

SNOWDROP.

I am just seventeen.   I feel so young ;
And yet I am already seventeen !

QUEEN (*aside*).

Would I were that age, too !

SNOWDROP.

                    What did you say ?

QUEEN.

Nothing.   And now, my darling, you must go ;
The King, your father, anxiously awaits you.

SNOWDROP.

I go, I go.   How beautiful these halls !
I think I shall be very happy here.   [*Exit.*

QUEEN (*looking darkly after her*).

Go, fool ! be happy then !   Your time is short !
I'll not endure this rival at my side.
Far rather would I lose all wealth and power
Than my renown of beauty.   She must die !

Enter a HUNTER.

I have commanded you.   Can you be true ?

HUNTER.

As sword is to the sheath, so I to you.

QUEEN.

Will you fulfil my slightest wish—command ?

HUNTER.

Queen, I would die, if death came from your hand !

QUEEN.

Can you be silent ?—for I know you're brave.

HUNTER.

My lips are silent as the gloomy grave.

QUEEN.

'Tis well. Now listen ! Above all, obey !
The hunt takes place to-morrow. Is 't not so ?

HUNTER.

Ay, Queen.

QUEEN.

The Princess is thy special care ?

HUNTER.

She is. What then ?

QUEEN (*slowly*).

Then *lose her in the wood.*

HUNTER.

Lose her ! What mean you ?

QUEEN (*impressively*).

        Lose her, that she may
Never return again.   Lose her, for good.
What! *Still* you fail to understand my drift?
Then I 'll be plain, and bid you murder her!

HUNTER (*horrified*).

I should do murder!

QUEEN (*disdainfully*).

        Is it the *first* time?
Beware my anger!

HUNTER.

        Call not that to mind!
An action done in wrath, repented sore;
But this delib'rate butchery—I'll not do it!

QUEEN.

How!—will not do it? Your fate is in my hands.

HUNTER.

What has she done? So young, and ah! so fair!

QUEEN (*aside*).

Her only crime—*the* one I can't forgive !
(*Aloud*) If you refuse, to-night I'll yet reveal
How young Hubertus found his sudden death.

HUNTER.

You are a fiend, fair Queen ; but I obey !

QUEEN (*joyfully*).

You're laying up a lasting obligation ;
And, rest assured, I never will forget you.

HUNTER.

Enough of this !   When shall 't be done ?

QUEEN.

>   To-morrow.

Leave me, now.   But as soon as she is dead
Come back to me, and claim your just reward.

>   [*Exit* HUNTER.

He is secure !   He will be true to me !
Ah, soon my vengeance dire shall fall on her !
I cannot live, I cannot sleep or think,
While she—the Hated—stands within my light !
Patience ! to-morrow I will ask again—
To-morrow celebrates my triumphs new !

>   [*Exit* QUEEN.

Enter Snowdrop *and* Prince Faithful.

SNOWDROP.

And so you wish much to accompany me?
But I am yon stern hunter's special care!
You could not scare the wild beasts and the snakes,
That lurk in yon dark forest. You are young,
And we might pluck the flowers upon the mead,
But much I fear that you could not defend me.

PRINCE.

Try me, fair Snowdrop, that is all I ask!
And if you deem me young, yet am I brave,
And sooner far than aught should threaten you,
I'd gladly lose my life, protecting yours!
Try me, dear Snowdrop. Look you, long ago,
I had a sister—she was fair as you.
I loved her well, and often we together
Have roamed the woods in yon past happy days.
One day, to gather flowers, she left our hut—
She went—and never to this hour returned!

(*Stopping with emotion.*)

I know not what it is, but some dark voice
Warns me to ask you humbly not to go,
Or, if you go, to take me at your side.

SNOWDROP (*gently*).

And have you never since heard of your sister ?

PRINCE.

I do not even know where lies her grave.

SNOWDROP (*kindly*).

Poor boy ! your fate is sad.   I'm very grieved.

PRINCE.

Your kindness, Snowdrop, soothes my wounded heart.
Oh, do not go !   Believe me, yonder man
Is stern and gloomy ; he would not amuse you.
Take *me*, dear Snowdrop, as your humble page.

SNOWDROP (*gayly*).

Oh, I don't mind his looks ; I think he's kind.
He told me he would show me gloomy dens,
And cataracts of foaming water.   Trees
So high that you can scarcely see the tops,
And many a startled deer and timid fawn.
I've never seen a forest !   Then he said
That I should hear the solemn song the wind
Sings through the leafy branches.   I will go.
Farewell ! fret not, full soon I will return,

And then we'll gayly wander o'er the mead,
And you shall tell me every flower that blows,
And you shall teach me every bird that sings.

                                    [*Exit.*

PRINCE.

Ah, dearest Snowdrop, may that wish prove true!

CURTAIN.

G

SCENE II.

A Forest.

Enter SNOWDROP *and* HUNTER.

SNOWDROP.

And so this is a forest?

HUNTER.

As you see.
Well, do you like it? Have I told you wrong?

SNOWDROP.

Oh no, it is a great and wondrous place,
But—but it is so gloomy and so sad!
No sunshine! Only swaying, sobbing trees!
I feel so sad! No birds are warbling here;
I fain would hear the singing, soaring lark,
Oh, take me back, it is too mournful here!

HUNTER (*aside*).

A demon art thou, Queen, yet I obey!
(*Aloud*) I cannot.

SNOWDROP.

What, you cannot?   Have you lost
The way perchance ?

HUNTER.

I have not lost the way.
I cannot take you back because I've sworn
To kill you here! (*setting his teeth.*)   I *will* not take
    you back!

SNOWDROP.

To *kill* me ?   Heavens ! have I heard aright ?
Ah no, ah no, you must be mocking me !

HUNTER.

Look in my face.   Do you see banter there ?
Perchance a hidden gleam of mirth you see ?

SNOWDROP.

Oh no, oh no !   'Tis clouded darkly o'er,
In dreadful resolution, fixed as death.

HUNTER.

Right thou discernest.   Therefore must thou die.

SNOWDROP (*falling on her knees before him, looks up*).

And have you really got the heart to kill me ?
They say that I am fair !   Can you destroy
My blooming youth, my young and tender limbs,
And never feel a pang of sad remorse ?
Ah no, your nature cannot be so hard !

HUNTER (*turning away*).

Young maid, I've sworn to do 't, and do 't I must.

SNOWDROP (*still kneeling*).

Oh, listen yet in pity e'er you strike !
Perchance you have a daughter, young as I——

HUNTER (*aside*).

I shall forget my oath if she talk thus !

SNOWDROP.

—Who loves, caresses you when you come home,
Who puts away your heavy gun for you,
Who decks the table bright with many a flower,
Who strokes your hair and sweetly sings to you——

HUNTER.

Stop, Princess!—Snowdrop!—I will hear no more.

SNOWDROP.

And you could doubtless also murder *her!*

HUNTER (*after a pause*).

Child, go thy ways! I'll never do thee harm!
And when thou prayest—also pray for me.
But, look you, Snowdrop! never dare return
Unto the palace, else we both must die!
The Queen, your mother, trust me, soon would find
A more obedient servant for her will.

SNOWDROP.

A thousand thanks, and blessings on your head:

Fear not, I'll lose me in this forest wild,
And never, never will I home return.

[Exit SNOWDROP.

HUNTER.

Ay, take that path.   'Twill lead you far from men,
And I, returning hence, will take another.

[Exit HUNTER.

Enter the SEVEN DWARFS.

FIRST DWARF.

It's time to go home,
  Our work is done,
The birds leave off singing
  When sets the sun.

SECOND DWARF.

We've dinner to get,
  And cook and dish;
I'm tired and hungry,
  I do so wish——

FOURTH DWARF.

I wish we'd a housemaid,
  I wish we'd a cook;
But what use is wishing,
She wont come by wishing,
  By hook or by crook!
And after my dinner
  I want my pipe;
Then I've got to wash dishes
  And help them to wipe!
It's very hard lines on a hard-working man,
To cook first his dinner,
To eat up his dinner,
And wash plate and pan!

THIRD DWARF.

We help, you know, brother;
  You don't do it *all!*

FOURTH DWARF (*discontentedly*).

I want a nice housemaid,
  To come at my call!

FIFTH DWARF.

But as we can't get her,
Suppose we go on.
Potatoes want boiling.
I think I'll run home.   [*Exit.*

SIXTH DWARF.

I must lay the table,
    And clean all the knives,
And polish the silver.
    I wish we had wives!   [*Exit.*

SEVENTH DWARF.

I've got to darn stockings,
    The heels are all torn;
I have to knit new ones
    From night until morn.

ALL DWARFS (*together, singing*).

We've too much work to do,
We've too much work to do;
We're hard-worked dwarfs, we want a housemaid,
    We've too much work to do!

FIRST DWARF.

Look here, boys! Don't you think we could get a servant? We ought to have a little comfort when we get home.

SECOND DWARF.

Right you are, brother. Somebody to warm one's slippers by the fire.

THIRD DWARF.

Ah, and to hand round our pipes and tobacco after dinner, and to give us our spills and matches.

FOURTH DWARF.

Ah, and to boil some water for our grog, and to mix it, and to slice the lemon, and to melt the sugar!

SEVENTH DWARF.

Wouldn't it be beautiful!

ALL DWARFS (*rubbing their hands*).

Ah, that *would* be beautiful indeed

FIRST DWARF.

But where are we to get her ?

SECOND DWARF.

Ah, where indeed ?

THIRD DWARF.

No one will come to live with us.

FOURTH DWARF.

It's a great shame !   Wages would be no object, one diamond a year and all found ; and I *do* so want a pretty housemaid !

ALL DWARFS (*lifting their hands*).

Oh, he wants a pretty housemaid !

FOURTH DWARF.

Yes I do—what then ?

FIRST DWARF.

I wait at table as a rule.   Don't *I* wait well enough ?

FOURTH DWARF.

Oh, you do well enough, but you **don't call** yourself a pretty housemaid, I suppose?

FIRST DWARF.

I don't know. What is a pretty housemaid like? I have never seen one, you know.

SECOND DWARF.

More have I!

THIRD DWARF.

More have I!

SEVENTH DWARF.

More have I!

FOURTH DWARF.

Well, I haven't seen one, either. But I know what she ought to be like! She ought to have curls, for one thing!

FIRST DWARF (*breathlessly*).

Oh, curls, ought she?

SECOND DWARF.

What colour, brother?

FOURTH DWARF.

Oh, golden, brown, or black—as she pleases.   Then she must have a neat little cap, and a smart apron with white lace-edging.

FIRST DWARF (*rapturously*).

A neat little cap !

SECOND DWARF (*ditto*).

A smart apron !

THIRD DWARF (*ditto*).

With white lace-edging !

SEVENTH DWARF (*ditto*).

Oh dear, how very lovely !

FOURTH DWARF.

Yes, that's what a pretty housemaid ought to be like, I think.   Of course she must be pretty, to begin with !

FIRST DWARF.

Oh, of course she must be pretty!

SECOND DWARF.

Lovely !

THIRD DWARF.

Beautiful !

SEVENTH DWARF.

Charming !

FOURTH DWARF (*to* FIRST DWARF).

Now, I hope *you* don't think *you* look like a pretty housemaid, do you ?

FIRST DWARF (*considering*).

Curls ? Neat little cap ? Smart apron ? Lace-edging ?—No, I can't say I do. I should *like* to, though !

FOURTH DWARF.

Ah, that's a very different thing !

SECOND DWARF.

But, really, we must go home now, or the others will scold us for being late ! Come on, brothers.

(*All* DWARFS *join hands and dance round slowly in a circle, singing*) :

We've too much work to do,
We've too much work to do ;
We're hard-worked dwarfs, we want a housemaid,
We've too much work to do !

CURTAIN.

Scene III.

Palace of Queen.

QUEEN.

How long he is!   What can have hindered him?
Would he were here to calm my jealousy!

Enter Hunter.

How now!   What speed?   Is Snowdrop dead?

HUNTER.

She is.

QUEEN.

Have you prepared a story of her loss?

HUNTER.

I have!   As, riding past a glen——

QUEEN.

Enough.
I know 'twill serve the purpose!   Have you hid
The body well?

HUNTER.

Madam, 'tis buried low,
And on the pine-tree 'neath whose solemn shade
Rests the Princess, I've notched three crosses deep.

QUEEN.

'Tis well! Now quickly tell me what I shall
Give him who executes so well my wish?

HUNTER.

I have one wish, and that is this—oh! Queen,
Dismiss me from your service even now!

QUEEN (*taken aback*).

Dismiss you? What? Look you, I cannot
    spare——

HUNTER.

Dismiss me, Queen, I say! Or, by my bow,
I'll go without permission, as I live!

QUEEN.

But why this hurry—this——

HUNTER.

Dismiss me, Queen !

QUEEN.

Shall I be safe ?   You know my secret, man !

HUNTER.

Think you, my head is not as dear to me
As yours is to yourself ?   Nay, fear me not.
I want no money, I need no reward ;
I want my liberty———

QUEEN (*quickly*).

Do you repent ?

HUNTER (*bitterly*).

Repent ?   Repent ! it is too late for that.
I wish to get me from your hateful sight.
Queen, fare you well, if that can be *your* lot !

[*Exit hastily.*

H

QUEEN.

A change of mind! He has repented him,
Like fickle man; he therefore turns on me.
Well, let him go. I'll bear his sudden loss.

(*Going to the window.*)

Ay, there he goes! He spurs his charger on,
And man and steed are both beyond my ken.
And now once more I am alone—my Glass
And I! Now I'll enjoy my triumph sweet!

(*Going to the wall.*)

My rival dead, I'm first! Ah, happy Queen,
Again thine own fair image shall be seen!

(*Draws curtain.*)

" Tell me, Mirror, I demand,
     Who is the fairest in the land ? "

                    (*Soft music is heard.*)

MIRROR.

" Thou art fair, but fairer far
     Than or sun, or moon, or star,

Is the lovely Snowdrop good,
Living with the Seven Dwarfs,
In the gloomy dark pinewood ! "

QUEEN.

Snowdrop again !—I fall !—I faint !—I die ! (*Faints.*)

CURTAIN.

Scene IV.

Dwarfs' Dwelling.

Enter Snowdrop, *timidly.*

Ah me, I am so weary!   Three long days
I've wandered through this forest wild ; my hands
Are torn with brambles ; sore and bruised my feet,
Berries and roots my only nourishment.
And that reminds that I am *so* hungry !
At length I've found a house ; who can live here ?
A table, seven chairs, and seven beds,
And seven plates, and seven forks and knives,
And seven glasses—oh, how very funny !
Oh dear, I am so tired, I'll sit down !
The table's spread !   That's good, I will begin,
And hope the owners will not count it sin !

(Commences to eat.)

What's in this jug ?   It's beer, I'll boldly swear !
I never tasted it (*drinks*).   Delicious, I declare !
And here is cheese !   I'll have some of that too.
A Princess—bread and cheese—vulgar, but true !
I think I've made a very passing meal,
I'll go to bed—how sleepy now I feel !

(Goes to the farthest bed and lies down.)

Enter the Seven Dwarfs.

FIRST DWARF.

My brothers, I'm hungry !

SECOND DWARF.

The same say I ;
The dinner is waiting.

THIRD DWARF.

Why ! who's cut the pie ?

FOURTH DWARF.

Who's sat on my seat ?

FIFTH DWARF.

Who's used my fork ?

SIXTH DWARF.

There's a hole in the cheese !

SEVENTH DWARF.

And a cut in the pork !

FIRST DWARF.

My bread is eaten !

SECOND DWARF.

Oh, what a bore,
The beer-jug is empty !

FOURTH DWARF.

Go to the cellar
    And draw some more.

FIFTH DWARF.

There's a leg off my chair !

SIXTH DWARF.

What wonder is that ?
You did it this morning.

FOURTH DWARF.

You're getting too fat !

FIRST DWARF.

There's a dent on my pillow !

SECOND DWARF.

My blanket is up !

THIRD DWARF.

Perhaps it's the kitten,
  Or the mischievous pup.

FIFTH DWARF.

It's too large for either.
  I cannot divine——

SIXTH DWARF.

Oh, come, look here, brothers!

SEVENTH DWARF.

There's somebody sleeping
  And dreaming in mine!
    (*They crowd round* SNOWDROP'S *bed.*)

FIRST DWARF.

Oh, what a fair maiden!

SECOND DWARF.

How cometh she here?

THIRD DWARF.

What lovely dark ringlets!

FIFTH DWARF.

Oh, *she* drank the beer !

FOURTH DWARF.

Shut up, you young squeaker !

SIXTH DWARF.

She opens her eyes !

SEVENTH DWARF.

A world of mute wonder,
And innocent surprise !

SNOWDROP (*looking round*).

Where am I ? Was I dreaming ? Who are you ?

FIRST DWARF.

We are the Dwarfs ; you need not be afraid !

SECOND DWARF.

This is our dwelling. Will you live with us ?

FOURTH DWARF.

I think, upon my word, she might do wuss.

SNOWDROP.

What does he say ?   I cannot make him out.

FIFTH DWARF.

Excuse him, dear,—it was a touch of gout !

SIXTH DWARF.

He's got weak nerves, the hammer's ceaseless bang
Causes him sometimes to indulge in slang !

SNOWDROP.

I see !   Well, gentlemen, I'm a Princess,—
Not easy, though, the telling by my dress !
A cruel stepmother drove me from home,
Three days and nights did I bewildered roam !
She thinks me dead !   Return I never may,
Then let me as your faithful servant stay !
Oh pity me, nor drive me hence again !
You all look kind.   Let me not plead in vain.

FIRST DWARF.

You shall stay with us
And cook the dinner,
And make the beds,
As I'm a sinner !

SECOND DWARF.

You shall keep the keys.

FIFTH DWARF.
To the cellar too?

FOURTH DWARF.

Who asked your opinion?
What's that to you?

SIXTH DWARF.

Can you cook and sew?

SEVENTH DWARF.

Can you darn a stocking?

SNOWDROP.

I never tried yet—
    Isn't that shocking?
I used to read novels——

FIRST DWARF.
But not in the day?

SECOND DWARF.

All novels are trash.

THIRD DWARF.

And that's what I say!

FOURTH DWARF.

What's your name?   Are you dainty?
I know, though, you are!

SNOWDROP.

My name is Snowdrop.

FIFTH DWARF.

How jolly, my star!

SIXTH DWARF.

You needn't clean windows——

SEVENTH DWARF.

Because there are none!

FIRST DWARF.

And now we'll have dinner,
    When your chattering is done.
They encircle SNOWDROP, *and lead her to table.*)

FOURTH DWARF.

We've got a nice housemaid,
　Oh bright happy day!
She'll warm all our slippers,
She'll cut our tobacco,
She'll mix us our nightcaps,
　She'll tend us alway!

(Singing.)

I'll have no work to do,
I'll have no work to do;
I'll smoke my pipe in peace and bliss,
I'll have no work to do!

SCENE V.

Dwarfs' Dwelling, as before.

SNOWDROP.

I am so happy here; the first time in my life
I feel of use.   The dwarfs are very kind;
They never scold me, but they bid me mind,
And never let a soul within the door.
Indeed, I never will!   I'll lock it to make sure!

(Going to door a knock is heard.)

A knock?   Come in!   No, stay; I surely do forget;
I am to bolt the door.   I'll look and see—but yet——

QUEEN (*standing on threshold, disguised as an old
pedlar woman*).

Any laces, my dear, any necklaces rare?
Some ribbons, a comb in your bonny black hair?
Here are soaps, scents, and brushes, and jewels so fine,
Just one look, my darling, and all shall be thine!

SNOWDROP.

Go away; I don't want any trinkets to-day!

QUEEN.

Just look at them, pretty one ; do not say nay !
You are living alone with these gloomy old trees,
You'll not oft have a chance of such bargains as these.

SNOWDROP.

What's the price of that comb ? (*pointing.*)

QUEEN.

Now, please, let me in.

SNOWDROP.

No, no, I have promised !   To admit you were sin !

QUEEN.

Heighty-teighty ! how can an old woman alarm ?
Indeed, pretty chicken, I'll do you no harm !

SNOWDROP.

No matter, I've promised ; do you keep outside.

QUEEN.

I'll not go till this comb in your ringlets I've tried !

I will not come in! Here, just stoop down your
head.

(SNOWDROP *hesitates. At length she bends her
head. The* QUEEN *puts in the poisoned comb,
and* SNOWDROP *falls lifeless to ground.*)

QUEEN.

Aha! my fair maiden, at last you are dead!
At last I can triumph, at last I rejoice!
My enemy's vanquished——

Enter PRINCE FAITHFUL.

PRINCE FAITHFUL.

Ha! whose is that voice?

QUEEN.

You here, my fair boy? Ah, your errand I guess!

PRINCE FAITHFUL.

I've followed you miles, Queen, to find the Princess.
Where is she? I vow you shall tell me this day;
For she cannot be dead, as the people all say.

QUEEN (*scornfully*).

What a valiant knight ! It were pity to tell—
Look, then, at yon maiden, and notice her well.

PRINCE.

It is she ! It is Snowdrop ! so fair and so young ;
Stand—answer—false Queen ! you have done her foul
    wrong !

QUEEN.

What matters to you what I did or did not ?
I have crushed the young viper ! I leave the glad
    spot !   [*Exit.*

PRINCE (*kneeling beside* SNOWDROP).

Oh thou so fair, so lovely, and so good !
Why do I find thee thus ? I've sought thee out,
And after days of wandering, at length
I come on thy fair form, the spirit fled !
What use to tell thee now that I do love thee,
That I'm a noble Prince, and not a page,
Who only came into thy father's realm
For love of thee ? But all is now too late !

Oh! woe is me, that thou art dead and gone,
And woe is me, that I did love thee so,
And woe is me, that I do love thee still!
I'll go and seek some aid ; perchance a ray
Of hope may still return to comfort me !

> [*Exit* PRINCE.

Re-enter QUEEN, *drawing forth Glass from her basket.*

QUEEN.

He's gone! I am alone! I cannot wait,
But here, in my dead rival's presence, I
Will ask my Mirror for the answer glad !
At length assured before the Glass I tread ;
It will not, surely, dare reflect the dead !

> (*Addresses Mirror.*

" Mirror, tell me, I demand,
Who is the fairest in the land ? "

> (*A mournful strain of music.*)

MIRROR (*slowly*).

" Many are beautiful and fair ;
But of all the beauties rare
None can with thee, Queen, compare! "

I

QUEEN (*joyfully*).

At last!
Mirror, I thank thee from my heart,
A servant leal and true thou art!
Thou givest the answer I love best;
Now is my jealous heart at rest.

CURTAIN.

SCENE VI.

In the forest. Snowdrop *lies in state.* The Seven Dwarfs *are sitting or reclining round her bier.*

FIRST DWARF.

We've lost her, oh, brothers,
    Her spirit is fled !

SECOND DWARF.

Her cheeks are still rosy,
    She looks not like dead.

THIRD DWARF *(scattering flowers on her).*

I've gathered pale flowers,
    That bloom in the wood,
To scatter upon her,
    So fair and so good.

FOURTH DWARF.

The birds of the forest
    All weep at her shrine ;
The nightingale mourneth
    A requiem divine.

FIFTH DWARF.

She shall not be buried!

SIXTH DWARF.

She shall ever lie so!

SEVENTH DWARF.

Thus still we may see her,
'Twill lessen our woe!

Enter PRINCE FAITHFUL (*sadly*).

FOURTH DWARF.

Who's *he*, to come snivelling,
And making a fuss?
I'm sure all the mourning
Is well done by us.

FIRST DWARF.

Keep quiet, you grumbler,
Why should he not weep?
Perhaps he has known her—
His sorrow seems deep.

PRINCE.

Drive me not hence! My anguish is sincere!
Here lies fair Snowdrop, whom I sought so long;
And when, at length, I found her, lo, behold!
Her sweet eyes closed, her body stiff and cold.

FOURTH DWARF.

Pray, were you a suitor?
How came you in here?

THIRD DWARF.

She long was our servant,
We all held her dear.

FIRST DWARF.

She mended our stockings,
And darned up the heels.

SIXTH DWARF.

She cooked, oh, so nicely,
And dished up our meals!

SEVENTH DWARF.

She swept and she dusted
With carefullest eye!

FOURTH DWARF.

None drew the beer like her
    To make it froth high.

PRINCE.

I know she was a kind and gentle maid;
None, none can tell the bitter grief I feel!
I cannot live without her, even dead.
I pray you, friends, kind dwarfs, oh! pity me,
And let me bear her to my royal realm.
I'll give you anything you ask for her.
I tell you I must always see her face!

FIRST DWARF.

Well, so do *we* want her.

SECOND DWARF.

Do you think we've no heart?

THIRD DWARF.

My eyes are quite red
    From the tears' briny smart!

FOURTH DWARF.

I'm quite hoarse with weeping!

FIFTH DWARF.

My appetite's gone !

SIXTH DWARF.

My cries ought to soften
Or marble or stone !

PRINCE.

I doubt it not.   And yet I do entreat
To let me carry Snowdrop to my realm !
I'll place her in a crystal coffin there,
Within a hall of marble.   Flowers sweet
Shall ever grow around her resting-place ;
Not mournful cypress, or the solemn yew,
But clustering roses, laughing, fair as she,
While silver fountains plash in cadence soft.
I pray you, friends, to leave her unto me !

FIRST DWARF.

As thou seemest so anxious—

SECOND DWARF.

Why, take her away !

THIRD DWARF.

Although we shall miss her
For many a day.

PRINCE.

A thousand thanks, kind dwarfs!   I stand rebuked
Before your princely generosity.
Believe me, that I shall not prove ungrateful.
Have you a robe or shawl wherein to place her?

> (*He moves* SNOWDROP *in his arms, when her comb
> falls out of her hair.   She wakes, moves,
> and says, dreamily—*

SNOWDROP.

Where is she gone ?   I did not let her in!
Indeed, I did not mean to break my word !

PRINCE.

Who spoke?   Why, not—it could not have been Snowdrop !

SNOWDROP (*sitting up : still dreamily*).

I do not see her now ; perchance she's gone—
A bad, bad woman, almost like the Queen !

DWARFS (*all together*).

Snowdrop! Look up! You're safe! You are with
us !

PRINCE (*joyfully*).

Wake up, dear Snowdrop ; wake, and look on me !

SNOWDROP.

Oh joy ! on *you !* I deemed you far away !
How came you hither in this forest wild ?

PRINCE.

Where you can go, there can I follow too !

SNOWDROP (*alarmed*).

Oh speak ! you have not come to take me back ?

PRINCE.

My dearest wish is that you come with me.

SNOWDROP.

My stepmother will surely kill me then !

PRINCE.

Yes, Snowdrop, there ! But not within my realm.
There I shall guard, protect, and keep you safe,

If you will come with me and be my queen.
Say that you will; say that you love me, dear!

SNOWDROP.

I love you very much!   I'll go with you.

FOURTH DWARF.

And leave us for ever,
    Ungratefullest maid?
Pray, who gave you shelter
    When you were afraid?

SEVENTH DWARF.

Don't teaze! don't you see now
    How happy she is?

FOURTH DWARF.

I hate the young fellow,
    With his unshaven phiz!

PRINCE.

Come, dearest Snowdrop, ere the night descend,
Soon shalt thou enter my ancestral hall,
And all the land shall welcome thee as Queen.

SNOWDROP.

Good-bye, dear dwarfs, I never shall forget
Your kindness to a houseless, wandering child !

DWARFS.

Go, Snowdrop, and be happy.   We shall miss you ;
But go in peace ! the dwarfs do wish you well !

[*Exeunt* SNOWDROP *and* PRINCE FAITHFUL.

FOURTH DWARF (*sitting down and crying*).

Boohoo !   I'm so wretched!
I loved her so dear !
Who'll run for the future
And draw me my beer ?

CURTAIN.

Scene VII.

Queen's Palace.

QUEEN.

A year has passed ; my mind has been at peace.
To-day I hear a hostile rumour say
That none's so fair as our young neighbouring queen.
To know the truth of this I've hither come
To ask my Glass.   Why do I tremble thus ?

> (*Draws curtain, and asks eagerly :*)

> " Mirror, tell me, I demand,
>   Who is the fairest in the land ? "

> > (*Music.*)

MIRROR.

> " I answer well, I answer true,
>   Snowdrop is fairer far than you ! "

QUEEN.

What ! Snowdrop ?   Never !   She again alive ?

Enter the SEVEN DWARFS.

Whence swarm these imps like bees from out a hive?

(*The* DWARFS *form a circle round her, and prevent her getting out.*)

FIRST DWARF.

We've come to fetch you.

SECOND DWARF.

We want our Glass.

QUEEN (*angrily*).

My magic Mirror?
   Here's a nice pass!
Come, hands off, quickly!

FOURTH DWARF.

Excuse us, Queen;
Don't think to escape us,
   We're not so green!

QUEEN (*frightened*).
What do you want?

FIFTH DWARF.

To punish your crimes.

SIXTH DWARF.

You are our prisoner.

SEVENTH DWARF.

You'll see all betimes.

QUEEN.

Help! help! oh, my husband!

FIRST DWARF.

He'll lend a deaf ear.

.

FOURTH DWARF (*grinning*).

He'll be but too happy
  To lose you, my dear!

SEVENTH DWARF.

So come, let us take her—
  Forget not the Glass!
She'll ne'er have another.

FOURTH DWARF.

Do you hear that, my lass?

ALL.

We'll keep her imprisoned
In a lonely high tower,
Where no one shall see her
From this present hour !

(QUEEN *falls on her knees in despair.* DWARFS
*dance round her, while curtain slowly
falls.*)

Act 1.—Scene 1.
(Solo.)

(A faint strain of music.)

Music by K. C. Field.

PIANO.

Moderato.

pp

Slower. MIRROR. RECIT.

Thou the fair - est usedst to be, An - o - ther

fair - er now than thee; Love-ly Snowdrop, it is she.

Act 2.—Scene 2.

(Who is the fairest in the land.)

Lightly & trippingly.

MIRROR.

Thou art fair, but fair - er far Than or sun, or moon, or star,

Love - ly Snow-drop good,   Love - ly Snow-drop good,

Love - ly Snow - drop good,   Is the

love - ly Snowdrop good,

Snow-drop good, ... Snow-drop good.

8

Act 2.—Scene 5.

(A mournful strain of music.)

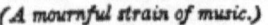

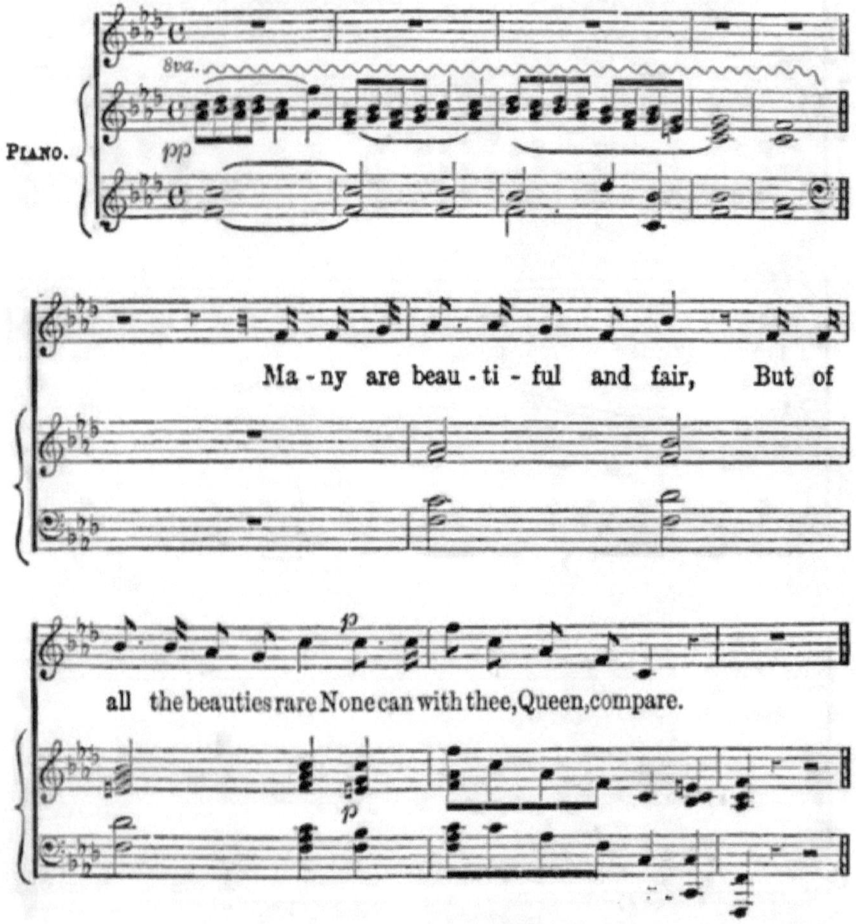
PIANO.
8va.
pp
Ma - ny are beau - ti - ful and fair, But of
p
all the beauties rare None can with thee, Queen, compare.
p

Act 3.—Scene 2.

Briskly. (In the land.)
rall.
I an-swer well, I an-swer true, Snowdrop, Snowdrop,
8va.
PIANO.
rall.

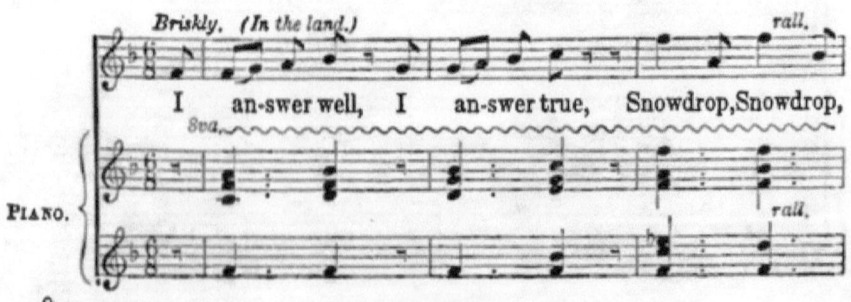

a tempo.
Snow-drop is fair - er far than you.
8va.
a tempo.

Act 3.—Scene 2.

(Chorus of Dwarfs in Unison.)

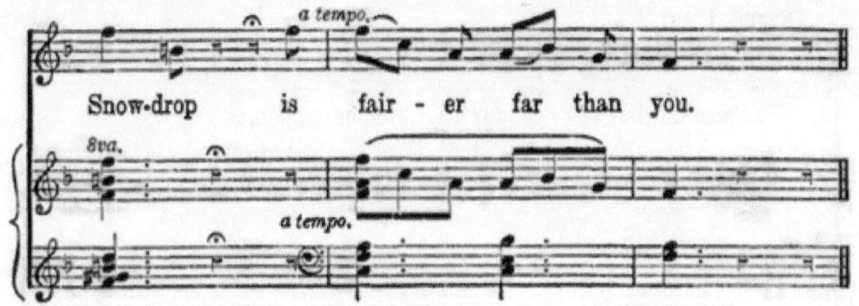

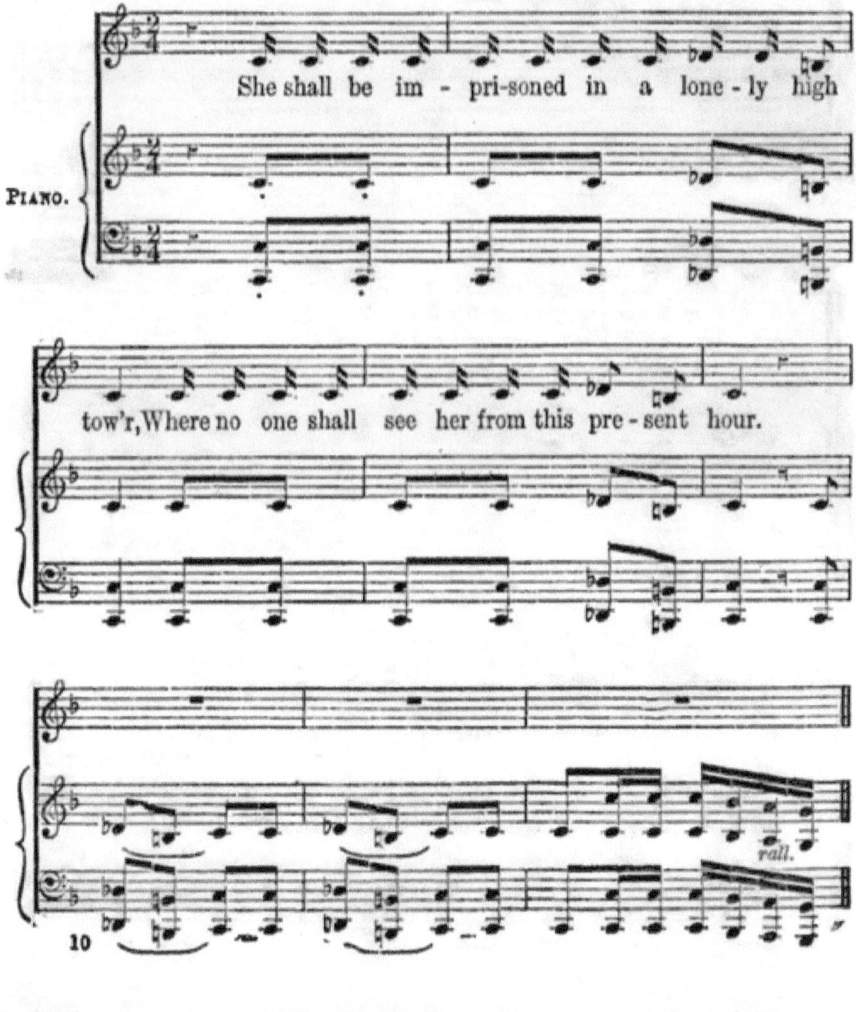
She shall be im - pri-soned in a lone - ly high
Piano.
tow'r, Where no one shall see her from this pre - sent hour.
rall.

CHORUS. *Vivace.* *f*

She was fair, but fair - er far Than sun, or moon, or star,

Is the love - ly Snowdrop fair, the love-ly Snowdrop fair.

She was fair, but fair - er far than sun, or moon, or star,

Is the love-ly Snow-drop fair, the love-ly Snow-drop fair,

11

Liv-ing with the se-ven dwarfs, In the lone-ly dark pine wood,

Liv-ing with the se-ven dwarfs, In the gloomy dark pine wood, In the

gloom-y dark pine wood.

Liv-ing with the se-ven dwarfs, In the gloom-y dark pine wood,

Liv-ing with the se-ven dwarfs, In the gloomy dark pine wood.

She was fair, but fair-er far Than sun, or moon, or star,

Is the love-ly Snowdrop good, the love-ly Snowdrop good.

She was fair, but fair-er far Than sun, or moon, or star,

13

dark pine wood, In the gloomy wood, In the gloom-y dark pine

In the gloomy dark pine wood, in the gloom-y dark pine

wood, In the gloom-y dark pine wood, In the gloom-y dark pine

wood, In the gloomy dark pine wood.

15

THE

BEAR PRINCE.

IN THREE ACTS.

INCIDENTAL REMARKS.

—◆◆—

THE scenery in this play is of so simple a character as to require no description, the river in the Third Act being of course invisible. The Costumes, too, of the different characters are not difficult; the Bear being clothed in furs and wearing a bear's head made of cardboard. Little Red Riding Hood, of course, must be dressed in character; while the Dwarfs look best in a brown or grey serge costume braided with red, their caps being of the same material. Hop-o'-my-Thumb should be played by a small, bright child, dressed in a long ulster, with chimney-pot hat and smart walking-cane.

Touching the animals, which play so important a part in fairy tales, it may here be suggested that the mouth of the actor, playing such a part, should *not* be covered by the mask, as the pronunciation is apt to become indistinct under the cardboard. These cardboard heads are easily procurable nowadays.

Dramatis Personæ.

—••—

SNOWWHITE.
ROSERED.
THEIR MOTHER.
LITTLE RED RIDING HOOD.
A PRINCESS.
THE BEAR (an Enchanted Prince).
HOP-O'-MY-THUMB.
TOADSTOOL }
SPIDERLEGS } Dwarfs.

THE BEAR PRINCE.

THE

BEAR PRINCE.

ACT I.

Interior of a Cottage.

Enter SNOWWHITE.

SNOWWHITE (*laying tea-things neatly*).

OW late mother is! And Rosered too! I hope she has not lost her way! She does not keep us waiting for tea as a rule. Tea is ready, and *I*'m quite ready, too, to begin. Let me see, is the room tidy and comfortable? Yes, I think it will do. How nice it is to look round a cosy room and then be able to say, *I* made it cosy and pretty! Oh, here is Rosered!

Enter ROSERED, *out of breath.*

ROSERED (*sitting down*).

Oh! oh! oh! I *am* so hungry! And where is mother? And is tea ready? And I've so much to tell you.

SNOWWHITE.

You naughty little puss, how late you are! Why, where have you been?

ROSERED.

I have been to see Red Riding Hood, you must know. And she told me such *lovely* stories, that I forgot all about the time.

SNOWWHITE.

I'm so glad you are home before mother is in. You know she is so anxious about you.

ROSERED.

How nice the kitchen looks! What a roaring fire!— and it's so cold outside, it's just beginning to snow. And how your tins and kettles glisten! it makes you quite warm and comfortable to look at them. What a capital housewife you are, Snow !

SNOWWHITE (*laughing*).

And what nonsense *you* talk, Rose dear !

ROSERED (*decidedly*).

I *never* talk nonsense — there !—oh, and Red Riding Hood is coming to have tea with us next week ! Do you think mother will allow us to ask Hop-o'-my-Thumb and the Princess to meet her ?

SNOWWHITE.

I daresay she will have no objection, if Red Riding Hood's mother allows her to come. But it's getting late in the year, you know ; winter is beginning, and then strange animals lurk in the forest. You remember what happened to poor little Red Riding Hood only last year ?

ROSERED.

Yes ! Poor little Red Riding Hood ! But *that* wolf was killed, you know.

SNOWWHITE.

That wolf was, certainly. But there are others, and all wolves are dangerous.

ROSERED (*reflectively*).

So they are. And her mother says she has grown *so* thin this summer—after the fright, you know—that she is obliged to give her cod-liver oil!

SNOWWHITE.

I don't wonder at it.

ROSERED.

Ah, isn't she good to take it? *I* shouldn't like to take cod-liver oil, should you? But she isn't a bit afraid of going out alone now. Isn't she brave?

SNOWWHITE.

So she is.   See—here's mother!

Enter their MOTHER.

MOTHER.

Well, girls!   safely home?   That's right.   It's snowing fast. (*Shaking her cloak.*)

SNOWWHITE.

I'm *so* glad you've come! You must want your tea.

ROSERED.

We're so *very* hungry, mother!

MOTHER.

Poor things! we'll have tea directly. Snow, dear, will you pour it out? I'll just hang up my cloak.

SNOWWHITE.

It's quite ready, mother dear!

MOTHER (*sitting down*).

Then we'll begin. Sit down, chicks—one on each side of me! That's it. Now, what have you been doing to-day while I was out?

SNOWWHITE.

I mended the stockings. Rosered, your holes are enormous, by the bye! How *do* you manage to tear your stockings so?

ROSERED.

Oh, I don't know. It's not *my* fault. It's the fault of the stockings, I think. Why do they *tear*?

SNOWWHITE.

Then I cooked the dinner, and then I washed up. And then I cleaned up the kitchen. Then I did my lessons.

ROSERED.

Oh, I forgot all about *mine !*

SNOWWHITE.

And then I got tea ready.   That's all.

MOTHER.

No need to tell you to do your duty, dear child.   And Rosered, what have you been doing, pray ?

ROSERED.

Oh, I helped Snowwhite washing up—and I broke a teacup—and I played with the cat—and then I went into the forest to gather wood—and then I went round to Red Riding Hood's !   And, coming home, I met three crows talking on a tree !

MOTHER.

Three crows ?

SNOWWHITE.

Talking on a tree ?

ROSERED.

Ay, three crows talking on a tree! I never heard crows talking before, either. So I stopped and listened. And then *they* stopped and looked at me. So I said, "Go on, crows! don't mind me!" And then they said, "Go home, you will have a visitor to-night!"

MOTHER.

A visitor ? Impossible !

SNOWWHITE.

Why, we live in the midst of a dense forest.

ROSERED.

Never mind—that's what they said. And then they croaked out this verse :

> "Snowwhite and Rosered,
> Strike not your suitor dead."

Oh, and that reminds me to ask you, mother—what *is* a suitor ?

SNOWWHITE.

Suitor? I never heard of it before.

MOTHER.

Suitor? Why—a suitor is—a—it's a—dear me, what ridiculous things crows are, to be sure!

ROSERED.

So *I* thought. And then I came home.

MOTHER.

Hush! What was that?

SNOWWHITE.

A branch tapping at the window.

ROSERED.

Perhaps it's the snow?

MOTHER.

No, it can't be that, I think. There it is again! (*A tap is heard.*)

SNOWWHITE (*getting up*).

Shall I open the door and see, mother?

MOTHER.

Do, dear. It may be some benighted wanderer, who has lost his way. See who it is, pray.

SNOWWHITE (*opening the door*).

Oh! oh! oh! oh! It's a big Bear! (*Runs back to her mother.*)

ROSERED.

A Bear! Oh, what shall we do?

MOTHER (*alarmed*).

A Bear?——

BEAR (*putting his head inside the door*).

Pray, do not be alarmed, my dear madam. There is not the slightest reason for anxiety, I assure you. I am perfectly well-behaved.

MOTHER (*doubtfully*).

Indeed! But we have been having such sad examples lately. The wolf, for instance, who——

BEAR (*coming in a little farther*).

Ah, but pray do not confound me with a wolf, my dear madam. Don't do me such an injustice, I beseech you. A bad lot are all the wolves. I would not touch a hair of yourself or of your children. All I ask is to be allowed to come in and warm myself. It's so cold outside !

MOTHER.

You seem a trustworthy brute. Come in.

Enter BEAR.

BEAR.

Thanks. You are very kind ; and those muffins do smell so nice!

MOTHER.

Come nearer to the fire. Don't be afraid, girls. It's only a polite and affable bear. He will not hurt you.

BEAR.

Not I. In fact I'm very fond of children ; *especially* of little girls ; *more* especially if they are pretty.

ROSERED (*to* SNOWWHITE).

Oh, I like him ! Don't you ?

SNOWWHITE (*to* ROSERED).

I can't tell yet, dear.

BEAR (*warming his paws by fire, sings*).

TUNE.—*Pretty little Polly Perkins.*

"It is cold in the forest, the snowflakes do fly,
And the fire blazed so jolly here, I'll go in, thinks I;
Do not turn me out, I pray you, for most truly I am
As gentle as a stupid turtle-dove and as mild as a
    lamb!"

MOTHER, SNOWWHITE, *and* ROSERED (*singing in chorus*).

"He's as gentle as a stupid turtle-dove and as mild as
    a lamb!"

BEAR (*politely*).

Might I have a muffin? I'm very hungry.

ROSERED.

Not yet, Bear. Sing us another verse! No song,
no supper, you know.

L

BEAR.

Very well.   Here goes.

"I'm a gentle, modest, loving Bruin, and I never
    touch meat,
But I rave for hot muffins and all things that are sweet,
Such as marmalade and cakes, and honey, and all kinds
    of jam—
For I'm as gentle as a stupid turtle-dove and as mild a
    lamb!"

MOTHER, SNOWWHITE, *and* ROSERED (*in chorus*).

"He's as gentle as a stupid turtle-dove and as mild as
    a lamb!"

BEAR.

Now may I have a muffin?

SNOWWHITE (*laughing*).

Indeed, you deserve your tea.

ROSERED.

No, not yet, Bear!   You must sing another verse
still.

For shame, Rosered! don't you see the poor Bear is hungry? He has been quite good-natured enough, I think!

ROSERED (*toasting a muffin by the fire*).

No, I'll not give him any muffins till he has sung another verse.

BEAR.

But, my dear, I can't! There's a painful void within me, I scarcely know where, but *somewhere*, and I really can't sing till that's filled up—I can't, indeed!

ROSERED (*offended*).

Very well then! Eat away! You seem to be rather greedy, I must say.

BEAR (*with dignity*).

I beg your pardon, Miss Rosered, but I was always considered a model of propriety; and I am *not* accustomed to be called greedy by little girls. (*He wipes one eye, carefully.*)

SNOWWHITE.

Oh, Rosered, he's crying!

MOTHER.

Beg his pardon, directly, my dear.

BEAR.

You are mistaken; I am *not* crying. Pray do not suppose any such thing. A piece of muffin flew into my eye, that's all.

ROSERED.

Oh, I am so very sorry! Do let me look, and I'll take it out myself. (*Examines* BEAR's *eye carefully.*) I can't see anything! (BEAR *winks.*) Oh, Bear, you are winking!

BEAR.

I can't help it. It's the muffin! But never mind now! let's make it up, and give me something to eat!

ROSERED.

Yes, Bear dear! And I'll butter your muffin my-self, and put the butter on—oh, so thick! Are you angry with me now?

BEAR (*taking a lump of sugar from table and sucking it*).

No. I'm very comfortable, thank you.

MOTHER.

Will you have some tea?

BEAR.

No, thank you; I have taken the pledge *never* to take tea!

SNOWWHITE.

Oh, indeed!

ROSERED.

Do take some wine, then! Snowwhite is famous for her wines. *Do* have some! There's her " acorn wine;" but we only take that when we have the stoma——

MOTHER.

Rose!

ROSERED.

Yes, mother dear—toothache, I mean. Then there's her daisy wine—ever heard of that?

BEAR.

No, I never did.

ROSERED.

I believe you.   And the best of it is, it *can't* intoxicate you.

BEAR.

I should think not.

ROSERED (*triumphantly*).

Ah, but *cowslip* wine gets into your head directly.

BEAR.

Does it, though ?

ROSERED.

Yes, and——

MOTHER.

You little chatterbox !   Supposing you fetch a bottle of this same cowslip wine for our guest?

BEAR (*hastily*).

Thanks, my dear madam, for your extreme kindness, but, strange to say, my thirst has entirely vanished.

MOTHER.

Then, children, it's bedtime. Be off with you! It's very late.

ROSERED.

Oh, please, mother, may we stop up a little longer?

SNOWWHITE.

I'm not a bit tired.

ROSERED.

I want to have some games and romps. Can you play at " Puss in the corner," Bear? At least, " Bear in the corner," it would be then !

SNOWWHITE.

Or do you know Blind Bear's Buff?

ROSERED.

I *should* like to give you such a drubbing, Bear dear !

BEAR (*amused*).

Should you ? Drub away then,—only recollect :

" Snowwhite and Rosered,
    Strike not your suitor dead ! "

ROSERED.

Oh, that's what the crows said to-night. And oh, mother, we *have* got a visitor after all!

MOTHER.

So we have! (*Aside*) I'm not afraid of *this* visitor, at all events! (*Aloud*) And now, to bed, to bed, to bed!

SNOWWHITE.

Where's the Bear to sleep, mother?

BEAR.

Let me lie before your chamber door. No dog would guard you better than I shall!

MOTHER (*taking up candle*).

Very well! Come on, then!

BEAR (*following her*).

This will be nice!

SNOWWHITE.

I'm so glad you've come!

ROSERED.

Good-night, dear old Bear! (*Gives him a hug.*) Dream of me, and be sure and don't snore!

MOTHER.

Rose! what nonsense you talk!

BEAR.

Never mind, madam, I rather like it, do you know.

(*Procession goes slowly out of the room; MOTHER first, with a candle; BEAR next; ROSERED and SNOWWHITE, with bunch of keys, last.*)

Enter TOADSTOOL *and* SPIDERLEGS.

(*They crawl on hands and feet from a corner of the room into front of stage, where they get up.*)

TOADSTOOL.

Spiderlegs!

SPIDERLEGS.

Here I am, master!

TOADSTOOL.

Are we safe? Look carefully round the room and tell me.

SPIDERLEGS (*going round the room*).

It's quite safe, master; they're all gone to bed!

TOADSTOOL.

How many are gone to bed?

SPIDERLEGS.

I don't know, master; I didn't see them go!

TOADSTOOL (*angrily*).

You Brickbat! you Badger! you bandy-legged Baboon! you belligerent Basilisk!

SPIDERLEGS.

Don't waste my time like that, I've got the knives to clean. What do you want?

TOADSTOOL.

You beardless Bigot! you beetleheaded Boomerang! you bilious——

SPIDERLEGS.

Very well, if that's all you want to say, I shall go; because I've heard it before, and I really must clean my knives.

Stop, I say! How dare you go when I am still talking?

SPIDERLEGS.

Well, I gave you warning. Besides, if you go shouting like that, you'll wake the people of the house. What do you want in this cottage?

TOADSTOOL.

I'll tell you by-and-by. And first of all—where is my big diamond?

SPIDERLEGS.

Don't know, and don't care. Haven't you got enough of them?

TOADSTOOL.

Never enough! Never enough!

SPIDERLEGS.

Well, *I* haven't got it! So don't say I have.

TOADSTOOL.

Yes, you have, you have, you have; I (*shouting*) know you have!

SPIDERLEGS (*shouting*).

No, I haven't, I haven't, I haven't, I haven't; I know I haven't!—Hush! we must not talk so loud.

TOADSTOOL (*in a stentorian whisper*).

Who began to shout?

SPIDERLEGS (*in a stentorian whisper*).

You did!

TOADSTOOL (*gradually getting louder again*).

I didn't, I didn't, I didn't!

SPIDER (*doing the same*).

You did, you did, you did!—Hullo, here we are shouting again! The people will certainly hear us.

TOADSTOOL.

Do you know why I have come here, Spiderlegs?

SPIDERLEGS.

Don't know, and don't care. I know you've crept and crawled through nasty damp tunnels, and I know

I've grazed my shins and elbows (*rubbing himself*). And I know that I've torn a big hole in my second-best coat. And who's to mend *that*, I should like to know?

TOADSTOOL.

You will, I suppose! And while you *are* about it, please mend this rent in my coat too—there's my marble-browed Moppet!

SPIDERLEGS.

Oh, I'm your Moppet now! Of course, whenever you want me to do anything, you can be polite! You called me a bilious Boomerang just now!

TOADSTOOL.

No, I didn't; no, I didn't, Spiderlegs! I said you were a beetleheaded Boomerang—and that's a very different thing, you know!

SPIDERLEGS.

Is it? I thought it was pretty much the same!

TOADSTOOL.

Listen, Spiderlegs! Do you know *who* is in this house?

SPIDERLEGS.

No, I don't.

TOADSTOOL.

Why, my enemy, the Prince, whom I have changed into a Bear !

SPIDERLEGS.

Well, can't you leave the poor animal alone? Haven't you injured him enough, first changing him into a Bear, and then taking away all his gold and silver?   And what a mean-spirited way of doing it, too!   You don't go up to a man——

TOADSTOOL.

How can I, my splenetic Spiderlegs? look at my size.

SPIDERLEGS.

You don't go up to a man boldly, I say, and knock him down, and take away his things in an upright and honest manner!   No, *you* go enchanting him, and then, when he's helpless, you go creeping into his house by way of mouseholes and keyholes !

TOADSTOOL.

Well, he's here, in this very cottage; he has sneaked into a worthy widow's family, I hear, and pretends to be *so* fond of the little girls—the hypocrite! But it doesn't matter! If he *is* fond of them, they'll never be fond of *him*, that's one comfort. He can never marry while he is a Bear; and trust *me* for keeping him one. Ha, ha! And now, my silver-voiced Spiderlegs, you sing the second verse of the song I have written in honour of his Bearship! I'll sing the first verse.

(*Sings.* TUNE.—*A Frog he would.*)

A Bear he would a-wooing go,
    Heigho! says Toady,
Whether his Master will let him or no;
With a growly, rowley, honey and cribbage.
    Heigho! says clever old Toady.

SPIDERLEGS (*sings*).

This Bear, he was a handsome Prince,
    Oh my! says Toady;
But a wee clever dwarf has made him wince;
With a growly, rowley, honey and cribbage
    Oh my! says clever old Toady.

TOADSTOOL (*sings*).

This stupid Bear, he began to spoon,
    Heigho ! says Toady ;
But we'll see if we can't put a stop to that soon ;
With a growly, rowley, honey and cribbage,
    Heigho ! says clever old Toady.

(They dance, and then crawl away again on hands and feet.)

END OF FIRST ACT.

ACT II.

SCENE—*Interior of Cottage.*

SNOWWHITE *and* ROSERED *are busy in preparing a tea-table.*

SNOWWHITE.

Why, how late it is, Rosered! The guests will be here directly, and we are not yet ready!

ROSERED.

Let me help you, Snow! Isn't it fun? Where is our Bear?

Enter the BEAR.

BEAR.

Here I am!

ROSERED.

Oh, you good-for-nothing, lazy animal! Come here directly. Lie down, sir!

BEAR.

Please, may I help you?

SNOWWHITE.

Ha, ha, the idea of a Bear helping! What with—
breaking the cups, I suppose?

ROSERED.

Or eating the jam?

BEAR.

Oh, do try me!

SHOWWHITE.

Well, can you lay a cloth?

BEAR.

Certainly I can.

SNOWWHITE.

Then let me see how you do it.

(BEAR *gravely lays white tablecloth, so that one
side hangs down more than the other.*)

Oh, Snowwhite, look ! He calls that laying a cloth !
Why, it's all on one side ! That's not straight ! Bear,
put it straight, or I'll——

BEAR.

Or, you'll—what ?

ROSERED.

Or I'll beat you ! There !

(BEAR *begins growling in fun.*)

ROSERED.

Oh, Snow, he's getting sulky ! This will never do !
Come here, sir ; I shall have to punish you, I see !

(SNOWWHITE *and* ROSERED *take a rolling-pin
and a wooden spoon, and run after him.*
BEAR *gets into a corner and pretends to
be very frightened, while the girls pretend
to beat him with their instruments.*)

ROSERED.

There, how do you like *that*, Bear ?

BEAR (*rubbing his elbows very hard*).

Very much, indeed ! Go on, please !

SNOWWHITE.

We shall never be ready if we go on playing like this! You must help me, both of you. (*Lays cloth herself.*) Now, where are the cups?

ROSERED (*bringing them from a sideboard*).
Here they are.

SNOWWHITE (*arranging them on table.*)
That's right. Now, where are the buns?

BEAR (*bringing two plates piled up with buns*).
Here they are, and don't they smell nice!

SNOWWHITE (*arranging them*).
That's it! And now the milk, Rose dear!

ROSERED.

There's the milk (*bringing it*).

SNOWWHITE.

Now the sugar, and then we shall be quite ready to receive our visitors.

BEAR (*bringing sugar-basin, from which he takes a lump and puts it into his mouth.*)
Here's the sugar.

SNOWWHITE.

I say ! Some one has been to the sugar (*shakes her finger at* BEAR). *I* know who !

BEAR (*penitently*).

It was only a little lump.

ROSERED.

Oh, you bad boy ! You'll catch it !

BEAR.

I won't do it again, please !

SNOWWHITE.

Here comes dear little Red Riding Hood !

Enter RED RIDING HOOD.

ROSERED (*kissing her*).

Oh, you darling ! I am so glad you have come !

SNOWWHITE.

How are you, dear ?

RED RIDING HOOD.

How do you do, Snowwhite and Rosered? Mother sends her compliments, and she hopes I will be a good girl! How do you do, Bear? Are you tame?

BEAR.

I am quite tame, my dear. You may kiss me, if you like.

RED RIDING HOOD.

No, thank you, sir. You see, mother says I must be very careful *indeed* how I meddle with strange animals. She is very anxious about me after that horrid wolf!

BEAR.

Naturally so, my dear! Still, I'm not a wolf, I'm a Bear, and I assure you I wouldn't hurt you! Would I, Rosered?

ROSERED.

Oh no, he's such a dear old thing! You may safely kiss him.

BEAR.

Just one little hug! I'll be very careful!

RED RIDING HOOD.

Well, as you know him so well, there's no harm in it, I suppose.   So I'll give you a kiss, Bear!

BEAR.

That's right.

> (RED RIDING HOOD *goes slowly up to him and kisses him.*)

BEAR *(gently embraces her)*.

Oh, this is nearly as nice as honey!

Enter HOP-O'-MY-THUMB.

SNOWWHITE.

Oh, here's Hop-o'-my-Thumb!   How do you do, Hop-o'-my-Thumb?

HOP-O'-MY-THUMB *(in a very high key)*.

I'm very well indeed!   Is tea ready?   Have you any buns and treacle?   Who's the gentleman in the fur coat?

SNOWWHITE.

He's a dear friend of ours, Hop, whom you have not yet seen. You need not be afraid of him.

HOP-O'-MY-THUMB.

Afraid? Who's afraid? Not I—stuff! I only asked in order to be introduced.

SNOWWHITE.

Bear! Allow me to introduce you to an old neighbour and playfellow, Hop-o'-my-Thumb. You may perhaps have heard of him?

BEAR (*bowing*).

Most happy, I'm sure, sir.

HOP-O'-MY-THUMB.

Happiness on my side! (*Aside*) Rough boor, it seems; wants my polish. Appears to be good-natured, though. I must draw him out a bit and put him at his ease. (*Aloud*) Do you attend the Opera, sir?

BEAR.

No. Do you?

I've not done so *yet*, but I *mean* to—I *mean* to! Been to the Derby this year?

BEAR.

No—have you?

HOP-O'-MY-THUMB.

No, I've not; but next year I mean to go—I certainly mean to go! Can you skate?

BEAR.

No—can you?

HOP-O'-MY-THUMB.

No, but I mean to learn—I certainly mean to learn. Do you like lollypops?

BEAR.

Rather!

HOP-O -MY-THUMB.

So do I. Let us be friends!

Enter the PRINCESS.

ROSERED.

Oh, here's the Princess! How good of you to come, Princess!

PRINCESS (*languidly*).

Yes,—I thought I would come round to see you. There being no ball at the palace to-night, I thought I would come here instead.

SNOWWHITE.

That is very kind of you, Princess.

PRINCESS.

It's a kettle-drum or a tea-fight, I suppose?

ROSERED.

I don't know. We only call it buns-and-tea.

PRINCESS.

It's the same thing, I daresay.

RED RIDING HOOD (*curiously*).

How did you come, ma'am?

PRINCESS.

Oh, as usual, little girl—with my brougham and dragon !

SNOWWHITE.

Come to tea, all of you.

HOP-O'-MY-THUMB (*to* SNOWWHITE).

Pray introduce me to Her Royal Highness.

SNOWWHITE.

With pleasure. Princess, allow me to introduce to you Hop-o'-my-Thumb.

PRINCESS.

Delighted—only I don't see him anywhere ! (*Looks over his head and passes on.*)

HOP-O'-MY-THUMB (*aside to* SNOWWHITE).

Stop a moment ! *What* Princess is she ? What's her name ? Where's her realm ? Is she married ? Is she rich ?

SNOWWHITE (*aside to* ПOP-O'-MY-THUMB).

Oh, I don't know, I'm sure. She's a Princess—like any other Princess, I suppose. We don't know anything about her.

ROSERED.

Do you take milk and sugar, Princess?

PRINCESS (*sitting down*).

Two drops of milk, please, and no sugar. A lump of gold, if you've got it.

ROSERED.

I'm so sorry, but we haven't any !

PRINCESS.

Never mind, then ! I ought to have brought it with me. Thank you, that will do nicely. Oh dear, you have put two and *a quarter* drops of milk in my tea ! I'm afraid I couldn't drink it, you know (*handing back her cup*).

ROSERED.

Let me give you another cup.

Thanks! Have you any diamond dust to sprinkle over my bread-and-butter?

SNOWWHITE.

I am afraid we have only jam.

PRINCESS.

Never mind, that will do for once in a way!

HOP-O'-MY-THUMB (*aside to* BEAR).

I meant to propose to Her Royal Highness, but I'm afraid her tastes are rather expensive.

BEAR (*aside to* HOP-O'-MY-THUMB).

Her bread-and-butter would mount up to something in a year, wouldn't it?

HOP-O'-MY-THUMB (*sighing*).

No, I'm afraid I can't afford it. But she's very handsome, and her style is superb. Heigho!

PRINCESS.

Well, here have I been sitting ten minutes and no one has said a word about my new dress! It's too bad! I might as well have stayed at home! I should at least have had a large mirror *there!* But it serves me right. Why did I go out to meet a company of *Dwarfs* (*looking at* HOP-O'-MY-THUMB), *Bears* (*looking at* BEAR), *and silly chits* (*looking at* SNOWWHITE, ROSERED, *and* RED RIDING HOOD)!

ROSERED (*aside to* SNOWWHITE).

Oh dear! she *is* in a temper!

SNOWWHITE (*aside*).

Say something to her, Rose dear!

ROSERED (*aside*).

I don't like to! Red Riding Hood, do *you*, please. All of us say something!

PRINCESS (*fanning herself indignantly*).

Well, can't one of you say a single word? You *are* a company of stupids, I must say!

NOWWHITE (*nudging* ROSERED).

Rosered, you say something!

ROSERED (*nudging* RED RIDING HOOD).

Oh, I can't! Red Riding Hood, *you* say something!

RED RIDING HOOD (*nudging* BEAR).

Oh, I am too frightened. Bear! you say something!

BEAR (*amused, nudging* HOP-O'-MY-THUMB).

Oh, I daresay! after the compliments she has been paying us all round! Bears, silly chits, and—— I say, Dwarf, *you* say something! Come, cheer her up! You are a lady's man, you know! I'm only a Bear!

HOP-O'-MY-THUMB (*sulkily*).

I don't care about her one brass farthing! I don't like being called names, I assure you! And I don't care if she knows it!

PRINCESS (*rising*).

Well, if no one will——

SNOWWHITE (*hurriedly*).

Oh, don't go yet, Princess !

ROSERED.

Have another bun, Princess !

PRINCESS (*disdainfully*).

Bun, indeed !

RED RIDING HOOD (*timidly*).

What a *lovely* dress you have got on, Princess !

PRINCESS (*appeased, sitting down again*).

At last !   It was high time, I can tell you, because I was just going !

SNOWWHITE (*to* RED RIDING HOOD).

What a good girl you arc !   (*Aloud to* PRINCESS) It is perfectly exquisite !

ROSERED (*aside*).

Now *my* courage is coming back.   (*Aloud*) And it *suits* you so well, Princess !

BEAR (*aside*).

I mustn't be behindhand either. (*Aloud*) It's the most perfect thing I have ever seen. (*Aside to* HOP-O'-MY-THUMB) Now it's your turn, Hop! Say something nice, there's a good fellow!

HOP-O'-MY-THUMB (*offended*).

No, I shan't! Why did she call me a dwarf? I'm not a giant, I know, but it's perfectly ridiculous her calling me a dwarf!

PRINCESS (*to* HOP-O'-MY-THUMB).

You haven't said anything yet!

HOP-O'-MY-THUMB (*curtly*).

Oh, the dress will do well enough, I daresay!

PRINCESS (*rising, and beginning to cry*).

Oh, he says the dress will do well enough!—oh dear, oh dear, that I should live to be insulted like this! Will do well enough! (*cries.*)

SNOWWHITE (*to* HOP-O'-MY-THUMB).

Goodness gracious! now she is beginning to cry. Whatever shall we do?

ROSERED (*to* HOP-O'-MY-THUMB).

You *might* have said something nice, Hop!

PRINCESS (*sobbing*).

The dress—will—will do well enough! Oh dear! oh dear!

RED RIDING HOOD.

Do say something nice, Hop—*do* now!

BEAR (*growling*).

What a nuisance these women are that are always crying! Hop, say something polite to her, now; don't stand on your dignity, old boy! Come on!

HOP-O'-MY-THUMB.

Well, as she is crying so hard, I suppose I've hurt her feelings. I'm so glad!

ROSERED.

Oh, Hop! for shame!

HOP-O'-MY-THUMB.

I meant to say, I'm so glad she's got feelings to
hurt; I didn't say I was glad I had hurt them!

ROSERED (*doubtfully*).

Oh, I see!

HOP-O'-MY-THUMB.

But as she shows a very proper feeling on the subject, I don't mind saying that I think the Princess's
dress is perfectly ravishing, enchanting, delightful, and
all the rest of it!

BEAR.

Bravo! Hear, hear! Encore!

PRINCESS (*getting up, and shaking hands with* HOP-O'-
MY-THUMB).

Sir, your sentiments do you honour! So you really
like my dress?

HOP-O'-MY-THUMB.

Like it? I think it's simply lovely!

N 2

PRINCESS (*giving him a locket*).

Then from this hour I create you my knight, and in commemoration of the solemn and joyful occasion I bestow on you my portrait in a locket! Kneel down!

HOP-O'-MY-THUMB (*kneeling down*).

This happiness is beyond my deserts!

PRINCESS (*putting locket round his neck*).

Rise, Sir Hop-o'-my-Thumb!

ROSERED.

This is beautiful!

SNOWWHITE.

How kind of the Princess!

RED RIDING HOOD.

I admired her dress first. Why doesn't she give me a locket too?

ROSERED.

Hush, dear!

BEAR.

Supposing little Red Riding Hood were to give us a song?

SNOWWHITE.

That would be nice! Do, dear!

ROSERED.

Oh, please do!

HOP-O'-MY-THUMB (*aside*).

No one asks *me* to sing.

RED RIDING HOOD.

But you've heard it all before!

ROSERED.

Never mind. That doesn't matter a bit.

PRINCESS.

Is there a Prince in it?

RED RIDING HOOD (*bashfully*).

No, ma'am.

Then *I* don't think much of your story.

RED RIDING HOOD.

I'm very sorry, but I can't help it.

BEAR.

Go on, little Red Riding Hood; we're waiting for you to begin.

(RED RIDING HOOD *goes in front of stage and sings.*)

TUNE.—*The Bailiff's Daughter of Islington.*

There was a maid, and a pretty little maid,
  And she wore a hood so red ;
And to this maid one fine morning
  Her mother dear had said :
" Now take this cake, now take this wine——"

HOP-O'-MY-THUMB.

Oh, I beg your pardon, but what sort of cake was it ?

RED RIDING HOOD (*speaking*).

It was a seed-cake.

HOP-O'-MY-THUMB.

I don't care for seed-cake. Why didn't you have a plum-cake? It's ever so much nicer!

RED RIDING HOOD.

Mother thought seed-cake would be better for granny to have, you see, because she is so old.

HOP-O'-MY-THUMB.

Ah, but plum-cake is nicer, all the same.

ROSERED.

Don't interrupt, Hop! Go on with your song, dear.

RED RIDING HOOD (*continues*).

" Now take this cake, now take this wine
    To thy grandmother sick, with speed;
And loiter not in the forest wild,
    And of thy steps take heed."

So she took the cake, and she took the wine,
    Her heart was in great glee;
And eke she put on her little red hood,
    So pretty then to see.

And forth she went to the forest wild,
  And the sun laughed bright and gay,
And the flowers they smiled, all red and blue,
  That grew upon the way.

And she laughed and sang, and she danced and ran,
  She forgot her granny old ;
When sudden she a grisly brute
  Before her did behold.

ROSERED (*breathlessly*).

Oh ! was *that* the wolf, please ?

PRINCESS (*sharply*).

Of course it was ! Any one can tell that.

ROSERED.

Oh, I'm getting so frightened !

HOP-O'-MY-THUMB.

Pooh ! a wolf is nothing to be afraid of. *I*'m not !

SNOWWHITE.

Go on, Red Riding Hood ! We want to hear you
finish your song.

RED RIDING HOOD.

Yes, dear. (*Singing*) :

"Now tell thou me, thou pretty little maid,
 Where dost thou go to-day;
And is it far? art thou alone?
 Or hast thou lost thy way?"

HOP-O'-MY-THUMB.

That's the wolf asking all those questions, I suppose?

PRINCESS.

Of course it's the wolf! *Do* make haste with your song—it's so long !

RED RIDING HOOD.

I can't help it, ma'am! I sing it as it has been taught to me.

SNOWWHITE.

Yes, dear; and very nice it is !

RED RIDING HOOD.

Well, then I answered him (*singing*):

"I am alone, but not afraid;
  My granny lives in the wood,
And I am taking her flowers fair,
  And cake and wine so good."

(*Speaking*) Then this is the wolf speaking again, you
know! (*Singing*):

" Then fare thee well, my pretty little maid,
  And be thou not too late!"
With that the grisly creature grey,
  He ran off at a rate.

" Now, granny dear, art thou alone,
  And art thou sick or well?
I've brought thee cake, I've brought thee wine,
  And flowers that grow in the dell."

HOP-O'-MY-THUMB.

I beg your pardon, Red Riding Hood, but I should
really like to know what wine it was.

PRINCESS.

Dear me, Hop-o'-my-Thumb, you are *always* inter-
rupting! She'll *never* get to the end of that song, I
do believe!

RED RIDING HOOD.

It was ginger-wine, I think, sir!

HOP-O'-MY-THUMB.

Thank you! It's just as well to know.

BEAR.

Go on, dear.

RED RIDING HOOD.

Where was I? Oh, I know. (*Singing*):

" Oh I am ill, sweet Red Riding Hood;
    Now come thou in to me,
  That I may eat the cake and wine,
    And thy red hood may see."

(*Speaking*) But this wasn't granny speaking at all, you know, but the wolf, who had swallowed her up, and then lay in her bed and imitated her voice. So I answered (*singing*):

" Oh! and why have you such large rough ears,
    Dear granny, tell me, pray?"
" That I may more distinctly hear,
    Dear child what thou dost say!"

" Oh! and why have you such large black hands,
    Such nails, so sharp and long ? "
" That I may clasp thee to my heart,
    In my affection strong."

" Oh! and why have you such a large big mouth,
    Such teeth, so sharp and white ? "
" That I may eat thee, Little Riding Hood—
    That I with them may bite ! "

ROSERED.

Oh, and *did* he ?   How dreadful !

RED RIDING HOOD.

You'll hear.   This is the last verse coming.

PRINCESS (*sighing*).

Thank goodness !

ROSERED (*to* SNOWWHITE).

Isn't she rude ?   We'll not invite her again.

RED RIDING HOOD (*singing last verse very slowly and distinctly*).

Up jumped the wolf, the horrid, greedy wolf,
    And he ate me up, hood and all !
And that's my story, children dear,
    Which did of late befall.

HOP-O'-MY-THUMB.

Is that all ?

RED RIDING HOOD.

Yes, I've finished now.

SNOWWHITE.

Thank you very much for your pretty song, dear.

BEAR.

Brava ! brava ! bravissima !

RED RIDING HOOD.

What does that mean, sir ?

BEAR.

What does it mean ?   Oh, it means that we are very much obliged to you.

ROSERED (*drying her eyes*).

What a d—dreadful shame !   P—poor little Red Riding Hood !

HOP-O'-MY-THUMB.

How did you get out again ?

PRINCESS.

I confess, the whole affair strikes me as being slightly improbable, besides being very commonplace and tedious.   No dragons, only a common wild wolf,— and no Prince to deliver you, I suppose, child ?

RED RIDING HOOD.

No, it was only a huntsman !

PRINCESS.

Ah, I thought as much !   No, I really cannot stand this any longer.   Good-bye !   [*Exit hurriedly.*

BEAR.

You have not yet told us how you got out of the wolf !

Oh, that was very easy. The hunter came in, killed the wolf, cut him open, and then I jumped out! It *was* so dark inside!

ROSERED.

And what became of your granny?

RED RIDING HOOD.

Oh, she crawled out after me! The wolf had not hurt her at all. But mother says it was a severe shock to her system; and so, last winter, when poor granny's asthma came on again so bad, she died. Mother says, that if it hadn't been for the horrid wolf she might be alive now.

HOP-O'-MY-THUMB (*reflectively*).

Ah, I've been in the inside of animals more than once, so I know what it's like! I've been swallowed, in my time, by a fox, a cow, *and* a wolf, successively! And at last I was inside a smoked sausage, four months up a chimney!

ROSERED.

Oh! is that really true?

HOP-O'-MY-THUMB.

True? Of course it's true! Don't I say so? However, my honour never allows me to remain where my veracity is doubted! Besides, all the buns are finished. Good-bye!   [*Exit.*

RED RIDING HOOD.

I must go home, too. It's getting quite dark.

ROSERED.

Are you going to be fetched, dear?

RED RIDING HOOD.

No; we are without a servant just now, so mother can't send for me.

BEAR.

If you will accept me as an escort, I shall be delighted to see you home.

RED RIDING HOOD.

Oh, that will be nice!

BEAR.

And, look here, Red Riding Hood! if you will get upon my back, I shall be able to trot home quite fast.

RED RIDING HOOD (*clapping her hands*).

Oh, this is delightful! I shall have a ride!

ROSERED.

Get up, dear.

RED RIDING HOOD (*climbs upon* BEAR'S *back*).

I'm up!

BEAR.

Are you safe?

RED RIDING HOOD.

Quite safe! Good-bye, Snow! Good-bye, Rosered!
Mind you come and see me soon! Now, Bear! One
—two—three—and away!

ROSERED.

Good-bye, dear!

SNOWWHITE.

Come again soon!

[*Exeunt* RED RIDING HOOD *and* BEAR.

CURTAIN.

o

ACT III.

SCENE—*A Forest.*

Enter SNOWWHITE *and* ROSERED (*carrying small baskets*).

ROSERED.

Come on, Snow, we are late.

SNOWWHITE.

Yes, we stayed too long gathering berries and flowers. I feel quite tired.   But we must go home now, because mother will be anxious about us.

ROSERED.

Snow dear, do you think our dear Bear will come back ?

SNOWWHITE.

I hope so.   When he left us in the summer, he said he must leave us; but he promised to return in the winter when the first snow should fall.

ROSERED.

Oh, I do so wish he would come back soon! I do miss him so!

SNOWWHITE.

So do I, Rose! But we must be going now.

[*Exeunt* SNOWWHITE *and* ROSERED.

Enter TOADSTOOL (*carrying a rod and line*), *and* SPIDERLEGS (*from opposite side*).

TOADSTOOL.

I shall try my luck fishing to-day, Spiderlegs.

SPIDERLEGS.

Yes, master, I would.

TOADSTOOL (*sitting down at side of stage and holding his rod into side wings*).

You go round the corner, Spiderlegs. I can't fish with any one watching me: the fish never bite. But don't go far, Spiderlegs, because I might want you. Come directly you are called—do you hear? I *might* catch a big fish, and then I should want you to help me.

SPIDERLEGS.

All right, master! (*Aside*) He'll catch some pretty fish to-day, I'll be bound !

[*Exit* SPIDERLEGS.

TOADSTOOL (*fishing*).

Spiderlegs! Can you hear me when I call ?

SPIDERLEGS (*behind scenes*).

I hear you, master !

TOADSTOOL.

I think I had a bite then.

SPIDERLEGS.

Did you ?

TOADSTOOL.

Yes,—but he's got off again !

SPIDERLEGS.

Sorry to hear it.

TOADSTOOL (*excitedly*).

Spiderlegs! make haste! come here! I've got one! Such a beauty! What a lovely supper he'll make!

SPIDERLEGS (*running in*).

Where, master—oh, where? Do let's see!

TOADSTOOL (*hauling in his line*).

Gently—gently—we mustn't lose him. Here he is!

SPIDERLEGS.

Why, it's an old boot, master!

TOADSTOOL.

An old boot? You are an old boot yourself! (*Lands an old boot on the stage.*) Well, I never! It *is* an old boot, and no mistake! I never knew old boots took to gentles. How came he on my line, I wonder?

SPIDERLEGS.

Haven't the faintest idea, master. (*Aside*) I never put it there myself, oh no!

TOADSTOOL.

Well, go back again, Spiderlegs.   Better luck next time !

SPIDERLEGS.

I'm sure I hope so, master.   [*Exit.*

TOADSTOOL (*fishing again*).

Spiderlegs !

SPIDERLEGS (*behind scene*).

Yes, master.

TOADSTOOL.

I *nearly* had a bite that time !

SPIDERLEGS.

Glad to hear it, master.

TOADSTOOL.

Yes,—but he's gone off again.

SPIDERLEGS.

They sometimes *will* go off again, master.

TOADSTOOL.

Spiderlegs! make haste! come here! I've got a
fish! Such a beauty! What a glorious dish he'll
make for supper!

SPIDERLEGS (*running in*).

Where, master—oh, where? Do let's see!

TOADSTOOL (*hauling in his line*).

Gently—Spiderlegs—gently! We mustn't lose him!
Here he is!

SPIDERLEGS.

Why, it's a tin kettle, master, and no fish at all!

TOADSTOOL (*angrily*).

Tin kettle, indeed! You're a tin kettle yourself!
What next? (*Lands an old battered kettle on stage.*)
Well, I never! It *is* a tin kettle after all! I never
knew tin kettles took to lobworms! However came he
on my line, do you think, Spiderlegs?

SPIDERLEGS.

Haven't the remotest idea, master! (*Aside*) I never
put it on myself, oh no!

TOADSTOOL.

Well, go back again, Spiderlegs! Better luck next time.

SPIDERLEGS.

I'm sure I hope so, master! (*Aside*) I'll run home now, or he may find out my tricks, and shouldn't I catch it then! 　　　　　　　[*Exit* SPIDERLEGS.

TOADSTOOL.

Now I've got a bite, and no mistake! Spiderlegs! Spiderlegs, I say! Where is the lazy rascal? Ho! you there! Wait till I catch you, that's all! And here's my line entangled in my beard! Oh dear, oh dear! The fish will have me into the water before I can say Jack Robinson! (*Struggles violently, but gets nearer to side wings.*) Help! Help! Murder! Fire!

Enter SNOWWHITE *and* ROSERED.

SNOWWHITE.

Murder!

ROSERED.

Fire!—Where?

SNOWWHITE.

What a dreadful noise!

What a funny little man dancing a jig all by him-self!

Dancing a jig, indeed! Funny little man! Ridicu-lous great geese, you should rather say! Why don't you help me?

What do you want?

What are we to do? And oh,—why do you tie up your beard with your fishing line?

Why do I tie up my—— Oh, these girls are simply *idiots!* raving, moonstruck lunatics! As if I had done it on purpose! Don't you see a big fish is dragging me into the water? Why don't you lend a helping hand, instead of staring and gaping?

Oh, let me cut it!

ROSERED.

Why didn't you say so before ?

TOADSTOOL.

Cut it ? Cut my valuable, long, lovely, silken, silvery beard ? Not if I know it !

SNOWWHITE.

Well, as we can't help you, we'll go.

ROSERED.

Good-bye, funny little man !

TOADSTOOL.

Stop ! What heartless little monsters you must be ! Leaving a fellow-creature in such distress ! Have you a pair of scissors ?

SNOWWHITE.

Here is mine !

TOADSTOOL.

Then cut the line.

SNOWWHITE (*cutting line*).

There, you are free !

TOADSTOOL.

Small thanks to you! You've spoiled my noble beard! Ugh! May the Big Bear of the Forest eat you up!

Enter the BEAR, *running and growling.*

Oh! oh! oh! here he is! (*Throws down his fish-ing-rod and tries to escape.*)

BEAR (*running after him*).

Have I caught you at last, you miserable little wretch?

TOADSTOOL.

Pardon, oh most generous, most noble Prince! Have mercy on me!

BEAR.

Mercy! What mercy had you on me?

TOADSTOOL.

Oh, pray don't eat me up! I'm such a mite of a morsel! See, there are two nice white plump, chubby chicks for you! Eat them! (*Runs off.*)

BEAR (*running after him*).

Silence! You shall not escape your well-merited punishment.   [*Exit* BEAR.

SNOWWHITE.

Why, it is our Bear!

ROSERED.

Oh, I am so glad!

SNOWWHITE.

But what did the dwarf mean by calling him a Prince?

ROSERED.

I don't know! It's all nonsense, I believe!

SNOWWHITE.

Look, Rosered, who is this?

Re-enter BEAR *as* PRINCE.

PRINCE.

I am no Bear now, but a Prince, whom yonder malicious dwarf had changed into that odious shape! Only his death could disenchant me, and at last fortune again smiles on me. I am what you behold. Dear

Snowwhite! dear Rosered! I wish to show myself grateful for all the kindness you have bestowed on me. Which of you will marry me?

SNOWWHITE (*in a disappointed tone*).

A Prince!

ROSERED (*in same tone*).

Oh, I *am* so sorry! I don't care for Princes, and I'm sure Snowwhite doesn't either! And I don't want to be a Princess, and I'm sure Snowwhite doesn't either! And, oh dear, how stupid it all is! (*Begins to cry.*)

PRINCE.

But, my dearest Rosered——

ROSERED.

I'm *not* your dearest Rosered! And now, of course, you are too grand to come and live in a cottage! Princes can't have romps and games, you know! Oh dear! oh dear!

SNOWWHITE.

All the fun is gone, now you have turned out to be a Prince!

PRINCE.

But really I cannot help it! What was I to do?

ROSERED (*despondingly*).

I don't know, I'm sure. How miserable I do feel!
Oh dear! oh dear!

PRINCE.

But when you are a Princess——

ROSERED.

But I tell you I don't want to be a Princess!

SNOWWHITE.

And I am sure *I* don't!

PRINCE.

Here's a pretty fix! What's the use of being a
Prince, I should like to know?

ROSERED.

Don't ask *me !* I'm sure *I* don't know!

SNOWWHITE.

You had much better have remained a Bear!

PRINCE.

And, pray, what am I to do with all my pearls and diamonds and gold, if you won't have them?

ROSERED.

I don't care what you do with them. Put the gold into the Princess's teacup—she'll want it; and sprinkle your diamond dust over her bread-and-butter! (*With a burst*) Oh, I *am* so miserable!

PRINCE.

What on earth am I to do?

ROSERED.

Go and marry the Princess, to be sure! We can't have Princes at our cottage, you know. That would be rather *too* absurd!

SNOWWHITE.

Your fine clothes would look out of place among our tins and coppers! Come, Rosered, we had better be going home! This is a miserable business!

ROSERED (*sobbing*).

Yes, we'll g-g-go home—and we'll t-t-tell mother!

[*Exeunt crying.*

PRINCE.

Well, upon my word! Is this the end of my enchantment to which I had been looking forward so much? Why, I had rather be a Bear again! This beats everything! When I was a poor shaggy animal they took me in, and fed me, and warmed me, and loved me, and beat me—ay! and kissed and pinched me, too—(*reflectively*) wasn't it nice?—and now I throw off my furs, and turn out a Prince, they actually go on as though their hearts would break. Poor children! *Children!* Ah, that's it!—they are but children as yet, after all, and that accounts for it. Why should I not humour them? I will! I will! I have it! Hurrah! Who would not rather be a happy Bear than a snubbed Prince? [*Exit hastily.*

Enter MOTHER.

MOTHER.

The girls not home yet? What can be the matter? I hope nothing has happened to them! But stay, here they come! But what do I see? Crying? Yes, both crying bitterly! What can be the matter? Such an unusual thing, too!

Enter SNOWWHITE *and* ROSERED (*slowly, and hand in hand, still crying*).

SNOWWHITE.

Oh, mother !

ROSERED.

Oh, mother dear !

SNOWWHITE.

We are so——

ROSERED.

We are so——

SNOWWHITE.

So very unhappy !

ROSERED.

So very, very, *very* miserable, you don't know !

MOTHER.

My dear children, you alarm me !   You are not hurt, I hope !

ROSERED.

No, we are not hurt, but——

SNOWWHITE.

When we were out in the f-forest——

P

ROSERED.

We met our Bear—oh dear, oh dear!

MOTHER.

You met your old friend the Bear? Well, there's nothing to cry about that, I suppose? I should have thought you would have been very pleased to see him!

SNOWWHITE.

Yes, s-so we were.

ROSERED.

Very pleased to see him we were, mother; but there was such an odious wicked dwarf——

SNOWWHITE.

And the Bear killed him, mother.

MOTHER.

But that didn't hurt *you*, did it?

SNOWWHITE.

N-no; but as soon as the dwarf was dead, the Bear turned into——

ROSERED.

A nasty, horrid, stupid Prince!

MOTHER.

A Prince! Is it possible?

SNOWWHITE.

And that isn't the w-worst of it yet! Then he asked one of us to-to-to——

ROSERED (*with a burst*).

To-to-to *marry him!* (*They cry bitterly.*)

MOTHER.

Is that all? And, pray, what did you say?

ROSERED.

We told him we didn't—we didn't—we didn't want to at all!

SNOWWHITE.

And that he should go and marry the Princess! But isn't it *dreadful,* mother dear?

MOTHER.

Very!

SNOWWHITE.

And now good-bye to our winter fun——

ROSERED.

And games——

SNOWWHITE.

And rides——

MOTHER.

Hush, you silly girls! Here comes the Prince!

Enter the PRINCE.

ROSERED.

Yes—here he is!

SNOWWHITE.

Look at him, mother!

MOTHER (*curtseying*).

I trust Your Royal Highness will excuse them. They are a couple of silly little chits, that don't know their own minds!

ROSERED.

Oh, don't they, though!

PRINCE.

Madam, it seems that my present condition is causing great trouble to your fair daughters.

MOTHER.

Pray do not be offended with them! They are so young——

PRINCE.

And so, to prevent any mistake on the subject, I once more make a last appeal! Snowwhite, will you be my wife?

SNOWWHITE.

What? And leave Rosered?—Never!

PRINCE.

Rosered, will *you* marry me?

ROSERED.

What, and leave Snowwhite? That I shall not! Besides, I don't care for *you* a bit!

PRINCE (*bowing*).

Thank you both for your candid answers. And so you do not love me?

SNOWWHITE.

No ; I can't say I do.

ROSERED.

I certainly don't !

MOTHER.

But, girls, how cruel !

PRINCE (*sadly*).

Then—farewell !   [*Exit.*

MOTHER.

There's a chance lost for you !   You'll never have such another !

ROSERED.

I don't care !

Re-enter BEAR.

BEAR.

May I come in now ?

ROSERED.

Oh, Snow, look here !

SNOWWHITE.

Why, it's our Bear !

BEAR.

Now will you love me as before?

ROSERED (*rushing up to him*).

Oh Bear—dear, dear old Bear! Will you really stop like this?

SNOWWHITE.

And will you remain with us?

BEAR.

I will remain like this exactly as long as you shall wish it!

ROSERED.

That will be for ever!

SNOWWHITE.

And a day!

ROSERED (*dancing round him and clapping her hands*).

Oh, Snowwhite, this is delicious! I *am* so happy!

SNOWWHITE.

So am I, dear!

ROSERED.

Oh, you darling, ugly, dear old Bear, how I love you! You are so much nicer than that horrid Prince!

SNOWWHITE.

So say I!

BEAR (*laughing*).

You are a complimentary set of young ladies, I must say! Give me a hug, girls!

SNOWWHITE }
ROSERED   } *fly to embrace him, one on each side.*

MOTHER.

Bless ye, my children! (*Aside*) He may change into a Prince again some day—who knows?

CURTAIN.

IT IS COLD IN THE FOREST.

By permission of MESSRS. HOPWOOD & CREW.

VOICE.

PIANO.

1. It is cold in the fo-rest, the snowflakes do fly, And the
2. I'm a gen-tle modest Bru-in, and I ne-ver touch meat, But I

fire blazed so jol-ly here, I'll go in, thinks I; Do not
rave for hot muf-fins and all things that are sweet, Such as

turn me out, I pray you, for most tru-ly I am As
mar-malade, and cakes and ho-ney, and all kinds of jam, For I'm as

Chorus to repeat line.

gentle as a stupid turtle dove, and as mild as a lamb. He's as gentle,
For I'm as gentle,

16

THERE WAS A MAID.

1. There was a maid, and a pret-ty lit-tle maid, And she wore a hood so red; And to this maid, one fine morn-ing, Her mo - ther dear hath said:

2. Now take this cake, and take this wine
   To thy grandmother sick, with speed;
And loiter not in the forest wild,
   And of thy steps take heed.

3. So she took the cake and she took the wine,
   Her heart was in great glee;
And eke she put on her little red hood,
   So pretty then to see.

4. And forth she went to the forest wild,
   And the sun laughed bright and gay,
And the flowers they smiled all red and blue,
   That grew upon the way.

5. And she laughed and sang, and danced and ran
    She forgot her granny old ;
  When sudden she a grisly brute
    Before her did behold.

6. " Now tell thou me, thou pretty little maid,
    Where dost thou go to-day,
  And is it far, art thou alone,
    Or hast thou lost thy way ? "

7. " I am alone, but not afraid,
    My granny lives in the wood ;
  And I am taking her flowers fair,
    And cake and wine so good."

8. " Then fare thee well, my pretty little maid,
    And be thou not too late ! "
  With that the grisly creature grey
    He ran off at a rate.

9. " Now, granny dear, art thou alone,
    And art thou sick or well ?
  I've brought thee cake, I've brought thee wine,
    And flowers that grow in the dell."

10. " Oh, I am ill, sweet Red Riding Hood,
    Now come thou in to me,
  That I may eat thy cake and wine,
    And thy red hood may see."

11. " Oh, and why have you such large rough ears,
    Dear granny, tell me, pray ? "
  " That I may more distinctly hear,
    Dear child, what thou dost say."

12. " Oh, and why have you such large black hands,
    Such nails, so sharp and long ? "
  " That I may clasp thee to my heart
    In my affection strong ! "

13. " Oh, and why have you such a large big mouth,
    Such teeth so sharp and white ? "
  " That I may eat thee, Little Riding Hood,
    That I with them may bite ! "

14. Up jumped the wolf, the horrid greedy wolf,
    And he ate me up, hood and all ;
  And that's my story, children dear,
    Which did of late befall.

A BEAR HE WOULD.

2. This Bear, he was a handsome Prince,
    Oh my, says Toady;
  But a wee clever drawf has made him wince,
  With a Growly, Rowly, Honey and Cribbage,
    Oh my, says clever old Toady.

3. This stupid Bear, he begins to spoon,
    Heigho, says Toady;
  But we'll see if we can't put a stop to that soon,
  With a Growly, Rowly, Honey and Cribbage,
    Heigho, says clever old Toady.

JACK

AND THE

PRINCESS WHO NEVER LAUGHED

IN FOUR ACTS.

INCIDENTAL REMARKS.

THE scenery in this play presents no difficulty whatever. The costumes are easy, especially the fancy ones. Of course the Chimney-Sweep, the Policeman, and the Clown must be in modern clothing, contrasting with the fantastic costumes of the other characters. The persons whose names have asterisks affixed may easily take another *rôle* besides their own. This play is more especially adapted for large families, or breaking-up parties.

The *Swan* is the only animal which would seem to present any difficulty to young performers. The best thing would be to *draw* a swan, life-size, on cardboard, cutting it out carefully afterwards. The bird must be gently pushed forward, either by Jack or Dame Trot, or Polly, and must, of course, be always presented in profile to the public. The few words which the Swan has to say may easily be spoken by Jack (in an altered voice), or by another actor concealed from the audience.

Dramatis Personæ.

———◆◆———

JACK.

* DAME TROT.

A SWAN.

KING JOLLY.

PRINCESS MELANCHOLICA.

* THE PRIME MINISTER.

SOBBINA ⎫
SNIFFINA ⎬ Court Ladies.
WIMPERINA ⎭

POLLY.

A CHIMNEY-SWEEP.

BURGOMASTER.

A POLICEMAN.

BURGOMASTER'S WIFE.

* PRINCE ORPHEUS   ⎫
* PRINCE GRIMALDI ⎬ Suitors of Princess.
* A CHRISTY MINSTREL ⎭

COURTIERS AND ATTENDANTS.

JACK AND THE PRINCESS WHO NEVER LAUGHED.

JACK

AND THE

PRINCESS WHO NEVER LAUGHED.

ACT I.

SCENE—*A Roadside.*

Enter JACK.

JACK (*looking round and whistling*).

WELL, here I am, travelling, like a great lord, for my own pleasure! I wonder where I'm going to travel to, that's all, because *I* don't know! After poor father's death, my eldest brother got the cottage and garden, and my other brother got the cow,

and pig, while I received nothing but this rusty old
chain (*pulling it out of his pocket*), and a padlock and
key! Very useful articles to a man who has nothing
to lock up! Then they wouldn't have me at home;
they said I dawdled about.—Well, perhaps I did. I
shouldn't wonder if I did. Next they turned me out and
told me to seek my fortune. Very well, who knows what
may turn up? I like travelling better than staying at
home. Perhaps I may find one of those hats which
render you invisible if you put it on. That would be
first-rate. What fun I should have! Or I may find
a lucky penny, that always leaves a golden ducat in
your pocket, whenever you turn it! Shouldn't I keep
on turning it, that's all!—And why should I not find
one, pray? Or, perchance, some fairy may take a fancy
to me, and give me one of those little tables which
serve up a dinner at a moment's notice! That would
be best of all, to my notion, as I'm always hungry.
I'm hungry now. Where's my crust of bread? (*sitting
down.*)   Hullo! who comes here?

Enter DAME TROT, *leading a* SWAN.

Good-day, mother.   Going to market?

DAME TROT.

Good-day, son.

JACK.

Where are you going to with him? (*pointing to* SWAN.)

DAME TROT.

Where you can never follow me!

JACK.

I say, don't you begin riddles before dinner, there's a good old soul! I'm never good at guessing them at any time, but before dinner—— Sit down first and share this with me. I've only dry bread myself, but you're heartily welcome.

DAME TROT (*sitting down next to* JACK).

Thank you. A crust is better than nothing.

JACK.

Right you are, old lady. I say, is that your Swan?

DAME TROT.

Do you think he is anybody else's?

JACK.

Look here! don't catch a fellow up as sharp as that! Of course I didn't mean that; but wouldn't a goose or a pig be more useful to you, now?

DAME TROT.

That depends!

JACK.

I say, old lady, didn't I give you dry bread just now?

DAME TROT (*looking at portion which* JACK *has cut, quietly*).

No, it's newly-baked bread, with a fine cut of ham inside!

JACK (*astonished*).

I have the same! I never!

DAME TROT.

Well—what are you staring at? Don't you know your own victuals when you see them?

JACK.

That's just it. I *do* know them when I see them, and I'm very certain I only put a piece of very dry bread in my pocket this morning!

DAME TROT.

Some mistake?

JACK.

Very funny mistake if it is—that's all I can say! I hope distress is not causing my mind to wander! I remember once, a long time ago, seeing a pudding when there was no pudding to see——

DAME TROT.

A kind of kitchen *Fata Morgana,* I suppose?

JACK.

But—(*scratching his head*)—I don't remember dry bread ever turning to a new loaf, with slices of ham in it!

DAME TROT.

Supposing we change the subject, Jack?

JACK.

Hullo !—how do you know my name ?

DAME TROT.

Oh, that's not difficult ! Every young fellow here-abouts is either called Jack, or Bill, or Jem ! I stumbled on the right name, you see !

JACK (*doubtfully*).

I *don't* see—however, go on ! What were you going to say ?

DAME TROT.

Where are you going to now ?

JACK.

I'm sure I don't know !

DAME TROT.

Have you ever heard of the Princess who never has laughed, Jack ?

JACK.

A Princess who has never laughed ? Ha, ha ! How ridiculous, to be sure ! Why, that makes me laugh.

I'm very easily tickled, I am ; and the mere idea of a Princess who has never laughed is very funny, I assure you.

DAME TROT.

The Monarch of the land, King Jolly, doesn't think it very funny, though. He is quite unhappy to think his only daughter should have been born under a melancholy star. He is a brother of old King Cole, you know, and, being very merry himself, he wants all his subjects, and more especially his daughter, to be merry too. But all in vain. He has a new plan every day to surprise her into a laugh, but it's no use. So he has issued a decree that the man who shall make the Princess Melancholica laugh shall marry her. (*Suddenly, to* JACK) Don't you think *you* could make her laugh ?

JACK (*alarmed*).

I make her laugh ! Goodness gracious ! What a dreadful idea ! I never did such a thing in my life !

DAME TROT.
That's no reason why you should not attempt it.

JACK.

Now, look here! I'll go anywhere and fight any-body at any time, with the greatest pleasure in life, or do anything else that is reasonable; but the idea of going up to a Princess and making her laugh quite frightens me! Don't mention it again, please.

DAME TROT.

Well, I won't. She's very beautiful.

JACK.

Very beautiful, is she? What a pity! I've half a mind—do you think I might tickle her with a feather?

DAME TROT.

No. The Princess must not be touched. You may try any other means but that one. And now I must go. As you were so kind as to share your dinner with me—I'll give you my Swan.

JACK.

Oh, thank you, that's very kind of you! But what shall I do with him? Can he lay golden eggs?

DAME TROT.

No.

JACK.

Ah, that's a pity! It might have been useful. Geese do that sometimes, I've heard. Can he lead me to places where treasure lies buried?

DAME TROT.

No.

JACK.

Then I don't see the use of your Swan, and that's the truth. Perhaps, though, he'll bring me my dinner every day, without my troubling my head about it?

DAME TROT.

No, he won't do that either.

JACK.

Then you may keep the stupid creature! I don't want a Swan dangling after me that can do absolutely nothing!

DAME TROT.

Jack, you are a foolish boy! You are refusing your own happiness, just because you do not happen

to see it lying before your nose. I will be kinder
to you than yourself, so I shall leave you the Swan
until you need him no longer. Take good care of
him, Jack, and he'll take care of you. Above all
things, do not allow any one to touch him; but if
they *do*, then call out—

> " Swan, Swan,
>   Hold on ! "

Now good-bye! and don't forget what I have told
you.   [*Exit* DAME TROT.

JACK (*looking after her, amazed*).

Here's a pretty fix! Why, she makes me have
him, willy nilly! I suppose I must take him now!
Wouldn't my brothers laugh if they were to catch
sight of me scouring the country with a Swan——

SWAN.

Better than with a donkey, any day !

JACK.

Hallo! You can speak, can you? Why didn't you
say so before ?

SWAN.

Because you didn't ask.

JACK.

Ah, your answers come pat. I suppose you've been to school?

SWAN.

About as much as you, I shouldn't wonder.

JACK.

Come, that isn't much for such a clever animal (*laughing*). Tell me, what do you think of me?

SWAN.

I think you are a fool, and, like many fools, destined to be lucky!

JACK (*jumping up*).

Come, I say, don't be rude!

SWAN.

I'm not rude, I only speak the truth!

JACK.

Look here, I don't want to be bothered with you! You go back to your old witch of a mistress. Go away, I don't want you, do you hear?

R

SWAN.

I hear, but I'm not going. You can't get rid of me, master, try as hard as you will. So you had better take your chain (you dropped it just now, here it is) and put it round my neck; then put on the padlock and lock it, and then lead me up yonder hill and down again through the wood. There we shall find a village, where the innkeeper is frying some splendid pancakes at this very moment!

JACK (*fastening chain round* SWAN'S *neck*).

Well, you are a funny creature! Obstinate, I'm afraid, but not stupid. I really believe I can smell those pancakes, Swan!

SWAN.

I can, master!

JACK (*smiling*).

Then lead on! I begin to fancy that my adventure of this morning is beginning to turn out better than I expected!   [*Exit* JACK, *leading* SWAN.

CURTAIN.

ACT II.

Scene—*Audience* **Room** *in Palace of* King Jolly.
Two thrones **are** *erected* **in** *centre of Stage,*
facing the *audience,* **on** *which the* King *and*
the Princess *seat themselves; their attendants*
grouping themselves suitably behind **and at**
the side of each throne respectively. **Care**
must be taken that the **Actors** *do* **not stand**
with *their* **backs to the** *audience; even* **the**
Prime Minister, *after* **the first low** *salutation*
to *Royalty, standing on left side,* **so** *that he*
may be seen *by* **all,** *while the Judges occupy*
three *seats, facing* **him** *on right side.*

Enter King Jolly *and attendants,* **and** *the* Princess
Melancholica *with* Sobbina, Sniffina, *and*
Wimperina, *also three Judges* **in** *wig and*
gown. The Princess **and** *her ladies carry*
their pocket-handkerchiefs conspicuously in
their hands. King *and* Princess *take their*
seats on respective **thrones.** *The* King *looks*

angry, while the PRINCESS *is very grave and indifferent throughout the scene.*

KING.

I am deeply grieved, daughter, to inform you that we have to deal with a case to-day which cuts me to the very heart.

PRINCESS.

Indeed, sire?

KING.

In spite of my severe laws and the rigid rules of the country, our long-trusted servant of State, the Prime Minister—you will hardly credit it!—was found last night writing an Ode to Melancholy! Conceive my disgust! An Ode to Melancholy! Not content with this flagrant act of disobedience, he was found sobbing —actually sobbing—over his own verses! "He was revelling in the luxury of an unwonted grief," he said. Unwonted fiddlesticks! Bah! I have no patience with the man! What do you say to this, daughter?

PRINCESS (*mournfully*).

I can hardly blame him, papa dear, I feel so much the same.

KING.

Alas! is not that my constant source of grief and trouble, ungrateful child? Do I not work day and night to win a smile from those pensive lips, those sad eyes of yours? And what is my reward? Tears and sighs, and sighs and tears! Was ever well-meaning monarch so dolefully damped? But I will persevere, and sooner or later, believe me, Melancholica, I will overcome even your mournful apathy!

PRINCESS.

I can't help it, papa dear! I sometimes *think* I would like to be able to laugh if I could, but unfortunately I *can't*, you see.

KING.

Very well, child. So you have said before. Don't say it again, if you can help it, please, because it only vexes me. Where is the Prime Minister? Let him be brought forth!

(PRIME MINISTER *is brought in, handcuffed and loaded with chains, which he clanks mournfully from time to time. He bows low to* KING *and* PRINCESS.)

PRINCESS.

Ah me, how happy the man who can suffer for his acts!

SOBBINA.

It's lovely!

SNIFFINA.

It's tender!

WIMPERINA.

It's so touching!

KING.

Ha! ungrateful and rebellious subject, do you see what your rash conduct has brought you to?

> (PRIME MINISTER *bows sadly and clanks his chains.*)

PRINCESS.

Methinks this jangling fellow makes soothing music!

SOBBINA.

Exquisite melody!

SNIFFINA.

Like the plash of fountains!

WIMPERINA.

Or the murmuring of waves!

KING.

One chance is left to you, if you will sincerely repent and apologize for your atrocious conduct. I am aware that I am erring, perhaps, through leniency, but, in regard to your long and faithful services, I am willing to make an exception. Do you repent?

PRIME MINISTER (*proudly*).

Never! Repent the divine promptings of the Muse? I would rather die!

KING.

Think again, ere it is too late! What! *you*, the first in the land—*you*, than whom none knows better the rules and decrees which you yourself have drawn up—*you* defy the laws to the unheard-of extent of writing an Ode to Melancholy! Shame on you! I can scarcely believe it!

PRINCESS.

Dear papa, I would so like to hear this same Ode!

KING.

Do you want to put me *quite* out of temper, child ?
Stuff and nonsense !

PRINCESS.

But, indeed, I would like to hear it so much (*coax-
ingly*). And my own papa has never yet refused a
request of mine.

KING.

There, there, there ! I am a weak old fool to humour
you, but I suppose I must. Prime Minister, have you
the *corpus delicti* about you ? Of course you have,
though—rather superfluous to ask, I fancy.

PRIME MINISTER.

So please your Majesty, I have. Only, as I am
handcuffed, I cannot get at it. It's in my doublet,
hidden near my heart !

KING.

Some one get it out for him. (*An attendant searches*
PRIME MINISTER, *and at last finds a big sheet of blue
foolscap paper, which he gives to him.*) Is that it ?

PRIME MINISTER.

It is, your Majesty.

KING.

Then read your trash, and be quick about it!

PRINCESS.

Papa dear!

KING.

Oh, bother it, I must relieve my feelings—and it *is* trash, I know! Judges, listen, attentively! You will have to pass sentence on what you hear.

PRIME MINISTER (*reading impressively and slowly*).

"To MELANCHOLY.

"Oh, sweet, sad night, with black and sooty pall,
   Come, shed thy melancholy o'er my soul——"

KING.

Most unnecessary request! What on earth do you want melancholy to be shed over your soul for, I should like to know, in the name of wonder?

PRIME MINISTER.

Sire, excuse me, but you understand not the higher yearnings ! (*reads.*)

"My wet eyes seek thee, and my sobs burst loud,
    But fall unheeded on the careless crowd."

KING.

The crowd isn't such a fool, I'm happy to say !

PRINCESS (*drying her eyes*).

It's *beautiful !*

KING.

There ! the mischief's done.   She's at it again ! (*resignedly.*)   Go on now with your precious verses, Prime Minister !

PRINCESS (*sobbing*).

Precious, indeed !   But do go on, please !

PRIME MINISTER (*bows, flattered, to* PRINCESS, *and goes on reading*).

"The miserable nightingale———

KING.

What! you don't mean to say *he*'s miserable too, do you? Oh, very good, very good!

PRIME MINISTER.

Yes, sire. You never heard of a *merry* nightingale, did you? (*reads.*)

"The miserable nightingale his mate
    Doth call with anguish, mingled deep with hate."

PRINCESS (*sobbing violently*).

Oh, oh, oh, oh! Weep with me, my maidens!

SOBBINA, SNIFFINA, WIMPERINA (*burying their faces in their handkerchiefs*).

We do, madam!

PRIME MINISTER (*bows again, and continues*).

"The moon looks livid, lurid, green on high,
    Then pour salt torrents from my wretched eye,
    And every breath comes laden with a sigh!"

KING.

Bosh! unutterable bosh!

PRINCESS.

It's perfectly lovely, papa! how can you say such a thing? Sobbina, a dry handkerchief, if you please, mine is drenched!

SOBBINA.

Here, your Royal Highness.

PRIME MINISTER (*reading*).

" Then let me weep my watery soul away,
And hide my tear-stained orbs from mocking day!"

That's all, sire!

KING.

That's all, is it? And quite enough too, I should think!

PRINCESS (*rising from her throne*).

Prime Minister, I thank you! Your Ode is perfect! There's not a gleam of sunshine in it from beginning to end! You will have to leave us soon—go in melancholy!

PRIME MINISTER.

Your Royal Highness could not pay me a more flattering compliment. I sincerely thank your Royal Highness!

KING.

Judges, you have heard the Ode! What is your sentence?

LORD CHIEF JUSTICE (*standing up*).

So please your Majesty, we find the prisoner guilty, without the slightest recommendation to mercy. We pronounce prisoner's goods and chattels to be confiscate to the Crown, and prisoner himself to be tickled out of the kingdom.

(PRIME MINISTER *clanks his chains violently.*)

KING.

Very good. See that it's properly done!
(PRIME MINISTER *is led out guarded, and clanking his chains.*)

KING.

And now, daughter dear, I must leave you. Business calls me hence. I have heard of a new invention called "Laughing Gas," which I must investigate. Ladies, I charge you to amuse the Princess!

[*Exit* KING, *followed by* JUDGES *and all his Courtiers.*

PRINCESS.

Are we alone, my friends ?

SOBBINA.

We are quite alone.

PRINCESS.

And unwatched ?

SNIFFINA.

Not a soul is near.

PRINCESS.

We had better be on the safe side ! Wimperina, do you lock the door !

WIMPERINA (*goes to door and locks it*).

Now we are safe, your Royal Highness !

PRINCESS.

Then away with hollow deception and mockery ! Let us cast off the sickly mask of mirth they would have us wear ! Let us be miserable ! Oh, I *am* so wretched ! (*Weeps bitterly.*)

[p. 247.

SOBBINA (*weeping too*).

I am deliciously low!

SNIFFINA.

I feel quite depressed! (*weeps.*)

WIMPERINA (*weeping*).

So do I, dear!

PRINCESS.

That is right!

SOBBINA.

If you please, your Royal Highness, we enjoyed our cry last night *so* much!

SNIFFINA.

Indeed, your Royal Highness, we have to thank you for a delightfully mournful evening!

PRINCESS.

I am so pleased you enjoyed it!

WIMPERINA.

Oh, above everything! There is nothing so nice as having a good cry, is there?

SOBBINA.

I hear it's getting quite fashionable in good society to invite an intimate friend to a cup of tea and a cry!

SNIFFINA.

Or a muffin and a sigh!

WIMPERINA.

Did you see the new pocket-handkerchief out? It's such a sweet thing! It's called the " Secret Weeper," but only the initiated know that.

PRINCESS.

Be careful, or our secret will be discovered. Only trusted friends may know. But my father must not even suspect it!

SOBBINA.

We are very careful, your Royal Highness. You have no idea how all the people are tired of having to smirk, and smile, and grin continually!

SNIFFINA.

They consider it quite a treat to be able to sit down to a good fit of the blues !

WIMPERINA.

Moping and depression are positive luxuries !

PRINCESS.

Still, be careful and secret ! If ever we be discovered, we shall be forced, in spite of ourselves, to be merry, or—what is that dreadful word my father is so fond of using ?

SOBBINA.

Jolly ! To be jolly, your Royal Highness !

PRINCESS (*shuddering*).

A dreadful word ! It's quite elevating, I declare ! And now we must go.—Sobbina, have you practised that Funeral March ?

SOBBINA.

I have practised and wept alternately, your Royal Highness !

PRINCESS.

Thank you.   And, Sniffina, can you recite my favourite elegy ?

SNIFFINA.

I have studied it with devotion !

PRINCESS.

Then I hope to hear it still to-day.—Wimperina, you will do me the favour of setting the Prime Minister's fine Ode to music, and singing it to me ?

WIMPERINA.

Your commands shall be obeyed with fervour !

PRINCESS.

Then let us retire to our private apartments.   We will have a regular, downright, tearful, crying, sighing, mournful evening !   Girls, let's make a night of it !

> [*Exeunt* PRINCESS MELANCHOLICA, SOBBINA, SNIF-
> FINA, *and* WIMPERINA, *slowly, and drying
> their eyes.*

CURTAIN.

ACT III.

SCENE—*Outside of a Wayside Inn.*

Enter JACK, *leading the* SWAN.

JACK.

So I am to stop here, am I? Very well, I have no objection to a glass of beer, as I am very thirsty! I say! Wanted, somebody!

Enter POLLY.

POLLY.

What did you please to want, sir?

JACK.

A glass of ale, and some bread-and-cheese.

POLLY.

Yes, sir, I'll be back directly. [*Exit into the house.*

SWAN.

Don't forget the rhyme, master!

JACK.

What rhyme?   Oh, I remember!

Enter POLLY (*with tray, jug, glass, &c.*).

POLLY.

Here is the bread-and-cheese, sir!   And the ale, sir!   Anything for the bird, sir?   You see our sign (*pointing to signboard*), "Entertainment for Man and Beast."

SWAN.

You are a very thoughtful young woman, my dear. It does you credit.

POLLY.

Oh, my goodness!   It's a talking Swan!   I never! What a nice bird!   Does he bite?

JACK (*pouring out some ale*).

Not that I know of.   If he does I'll muzzle him!

POLLY.

May I stroke him, please, sir?

JACK (*drinking*).

If you like.

POLLY (*stroking the* SWAN).

Pretty Swan! Nice Swan! (SWAN *screams loudly.*)

JACK.

Hullo! old fellow, what's that for? Oh, I know!

" Swan, Swan,
Hold on!"

POLLY (*is fixed to the* SWAN, *and struggles vainly to get away*).

Oh, *do* help me, there's a good man! I'm stuck to this funny bird! Do take me off, please!

JACK.

I'm afraid I can't help you. You *would* stroke him, you know. Pull hard!

POLLY (*struggling*).

So I *am* pulling hard, but I can't get off. Oh, for Mercy's sake, some one come and help me !

JACK (*laughing*).

Ha, ha ! Well, this beats everything I ever saw !

POLLY (*angrily*).

For shame, young man ! Do you call this a joke ? It's not pretty behaviour, let me tell you ! What have I done to you, that you should treat me like this ?

JACK (*still laughing*).

I would help you, in a moment, but I assure you it is out of my power. (*Aside*) I will see what this leads to.

Enter a CHIMNEY-SWEEP.

SWEEP.

Hullo ! what's the fun going on here ?

POLLY.

Oh, dear Smutty, you are an angel sent to help me ! Do help me to get away from this horrid bird !

SWEEP.

Is that all? Why, of course I will; if you don't mind my black fingers. Here goes! (*Pulls her by her left hand. SWAN screams loudly.*)

JACK.

" Swan, Swan,
Hold on ! "

SWEEP (*struggling violently*).

Why, what's this? I'm stuck too! Let go my hand, young woman, do you hear?

POLLY (*tearfully*).

I can't help it! I wish I could.

JACK.

Ha, ha, ha ! Well, this *is* comical!

SWEEP (*turning to* JACK).

All right, Mr. Jackanapes. Perhaps you'll go on laughing when I get free—that's all !

POLLY (*crying*).

Oh dear! oh dear! whatever shall I do?

Enter BURGOMASTER.

BURGOMASTER.

Highty-tighty, good people, what's all this about? This will never do. Disperse directly, I command you, or I will call in the Myrmidon of the Law.

SWEEP.

I only wish a peeler *was* here, your honour, and had brought his truncheon with him, to lay on some people! (*looking at* JACK.)

BURGOMASTER.

Do you mean to tell me that you cannot get away?

SWEEP.

Ah, I do mean to tell you so!

BURGOMASTER (*angrily*).

I don't believe you! It's a shameful hoax! You are an impudent set, the whole lot of you! But I will not stand it. Hi, officer!

Enter a POLICEMAN.

POLICEMAN.

Your worship?

BURGOMASTER.

Just take that Chimney-Sweep in charge. He's creating a disturbance, and says he can't get away! Impudence!

POLICEMAN.

Come, you move on, you know! What, you won't? Ah, then we'll see what a little persuasion will do, my fine fellow. (*Pulls* SWEEP's *left hand.* SWAN *screams loudly.*)

JACK.

" Swan, Swan,
Hold on!"

POLICEMAN (*struggling*).

Hi! I say, oh, come, none of your impudence! You let go my hand, will you? or it will be the worse for you!

JACK.

Ha, ha, ha !

SWEEP (*sulkily*).

Very good, peeler! I told you so.

BURGOMASTER.

What do you mean, officer? Are you in the conspiracy too? Why, this is a case of rank insubordination!

POLICEMAN.

Indeed, your worship, I can't help it! I *can't* get off.

BURGOMASTER.

Now my patience is at an end! I'll show you what it is, officer, to insult your superiors! (*Seizes him by the arm.* SWAN *screams loudly.*)

JACK.

" Swan, Swan,
Hold on ! "

BURGOMASTER (*struggling vainly in his turn*).

Murder! Fire! Thieves! I'll have you hanged, young man, when once I'm free, see if I don't! How dare you play off your tricks on me, the Burgomaster?

JACK.

Ha, ha, ha!

BURGOMASTER.

Fiend! villain! sorcerer! you shall pay dearly for this!

JACK.

Ha, ha, ha!

(SWAN *leads them, all struggling to get free, round the stage.*)

Enter BURGOMASTER'S WIFE.

WIFE (*clasping her hands*).

Goodness gracious me! What possesses you all, in the name of wonder? And why, if I may inquire, are you making a fool of yourself in broad daylight, husband?

BURGOMASTER (*grimly*).

Because I can't help it, my dear!

WIFE.

Can't help it! That's a pretty tale to tell to *me!* Do you take *me* for a fool, pray?

BURGOMASTER.

Don't waste your time talking, but give me your hand and pull me off! That would be more to the purpose. Officer! you are an idiot; and when I'm free I'll give you a month's hard labour for not understanding your duty better! Now then, wife, pull away!

WIFE.

I don't believe it! It's all nonsense! And I think, Burgomaster, that you ought to know better than playing such low practical jokes, at your time of life, too! (*Pulls her husband's arm.* SWAN *screams loudly*).

JACK.

" Swan, Swan,
Hold on ! "

WIFE.

What's this? I say, husband, let go my hand, will you? *I* am in no mood for fooling, if *you* are! Come, enough of this!

JACK.

Ha, ha, ha!

WIFE.

Ah, dear, young Impudence, you think it very funny, do you not? I'll tell you what it is, I'll have you put in the stocks, when once I'm free!

JACK.

Ha, ha, ha!

WIFE (*whimpering*).

Oh, husband, please to let me go, and I'll never be in a temper again, I promise, dear!

BURGOMASTER.

My love, do you suppose for a moment that I would stop here if I could help myself?—Young man, you wait till I get loose again! My anger is perfectly terrific! I solemnly ask you, have you ever seen an enraged lion?

JACK.

I cannot say I have.

BURGOMASTER.

Beware of *me*, then, when I am free!

WIFE.

Have you ever insulted a tigress ?

POLICEMAN.

Or heard of a snorting hyæna ?

SWEEP.

Or of an infuriated panther ?

POLLY.

Or of a wild catawampus ?

BURGOMASTER.

Are you aware that you can, and probably will be, hanged for this ?

WIFE.

Or starved in a subterranean dungeon ?

POLICEMAN.

Or larruped within an inch of your life ?

SWEEP.

Or sent up a chimney to choke ?

POLLY.

Or have your eyes scratched out ?

JACK.

Ha, ha ! It strikes me I have very excellent reasons for not letting you go.

Enter a CLOWN.

CLOWN.

Hullo, here we are again ! How do you do to-morrow, and how was you yesterday ? I say, though, this isn't quite fair, that it isn't ! You should have told me you were coming, too, and we might have gone somewhere else, my company and me. This is a sell; I thought we should be first, and here's another lot before us !

BURGOMASTER (*indignantly*).

Who do you suppose us to be, pray ?

CLOWN.

Something very much in my line, if I'm not mistaken, old gentleman ! Acrobats, or aeronauts, or——

BURGOMASTER.

Wretch! I am the Burgomaster!

CLOWN.

Happy to make your acquaintance, mate!

WIFE.

Husband, he calls you " mate " !

CLOWN (*to* WIFE, *suddenly*).

And how are *you*, my pretty dear?

WIFE.

Monster! I shall faint! He has called me a pretty
dear!

CLOWN.

Well, you are a lively company, I must say! There
isn't anything I can do for you, is there? No message
to send, or anything?

BURGOMASTER.

Good friend—— ,

CLOWN.

Oh, you are polite at last, are you? Well, I'm always fond of good manners, I am.

BURGOMASTER (*mildly*).

As I was going to observe, my good friend, you will doubtless have observed that an evil chance has thus bewitched us!

CLOWN.

You are a bewitching lot, I confess!

BURGOMASTER.

How it all has happened I am totally unable to explain. Let that young man (*pointing to* JACK) reconcile it with his conscience, if he has any, which I doubt. But if you will pull me off this bird, you shall have a five-pound note on the spot!

CLOWN.

And why didn't you say that at first, instead of calling me names? (*To* WIFE) Come on, old lady; you first, and then your husband! We'll have you both off the sandbank in a jiffey! (*Pulls her arm.*)

T

WIFE.

Oh! you hurt me.

(SWAN *screams loudly.*)

JACK.

" Swan, Swan,
Hold on!"

CLOWN.

Now I'm done for—all of a sudden, too! Well, of all queer starts! If any one should happen to see my sweetheart, be so good as to give her my love, and tell her not to wait supper for me. Will any one be so good?

JACK (*laughing*).

Certainly, if I see her.

CLOWN.

Thank you, sir.

SWAN.

You have enough now!

JACK.

I have enough, have I?

SWAN.

Yes; that will do nicely.

JACK.

Oh! And pray, what is the next move? What am I to do with my company?

SWAN.

You are to lead them all to the next town!

JACK.

At once?

SWAN.

At once.

BURGOMASTER (*politely*).

I think there must be some little mistake. The next town is forty miles off!

SWAN.

Just so.

BURGOMASTER.

But I've a particular engagement at twelve o'clock, and it must be that time now.

JACK.

You will have to put off that little engagement just now, I am afraid.

WIFE.

My dinner will spoil! And I have to give my cook warning this morning.

JACK.

I fear you will have to postpone that little scene of domestic enjoyment to another day.

POLICEMAN.

I can't go, that's flat. I've to take three fellows in charge!

JACK.

I rather think you'll have to take yourself in charge first, old fellow.

SWEEP.

I've got to sweep a chimney at a family where I've given my word of honour to be at a particular hour.

JACK.

I fancy the family will have to sweep their chimney themselves to-day.

POLLY.

Oh, dear ! I forgot all about the beer, and I remember I've left the tap running.

JACK.

As the cask is sure to be empty by this time, it's no use troubling to go to see about it, I suppose?

CLOWN.

Let's go! I *did* have an engagement too, but I think I can pick up some invaluable hints for the next pantomime. So it's all in the way of business!

JACK.

Then follow me! And if you should help me to discover my fortune, none of you shall repent this day's wild frolic!

> [*Exit* JACK, *leading* SWAN, *after whom, in a long row, come* POLLY, SWEEP, POLICEMAN, BURGOMASTER, BURGOMASTER'S WIFE, *and* CLOWN, *all grumbling, sighing, and crying.*

CURTAIN.

ACT IV.

SCENE—*Audience Room in* KING JOLLY'S *Palace.*

The KING *and* PRINCESS *again sit on their thrones side by side.* Attendants, courtiers, and ladies *are arranged as before, so as to form a semi-circle. The three suitors,* PRINCE ORPHEUS, PRINCE GRIMALDI, *and a* CHRISTY MINSTREL *are standing at the side, and each one comes forward as he is called. They must not, however, stand with their backs to the audience.*

KING.

The decree of our land ordains that any man who causes the Princess, our daughter, to laugh—nay, or even smile—shall gain her for his wife, and after our death reign with her over this kingdom. Say, Melancholica, is it not so?

PRINCESS (*sighing*).

Yes, papa dear.

KING.

Again I see three youths before me, who think that they can easily perform what no man has done yet. Brave youths! But, much I fear me, doomed to disappointment! Speak, Prince Orpheus, for you are the first on the list. Therefore come forward, and try your fortune!

PRINCE ORPHEUS.

I am all eagerness to try, your Majesty. The Princess Melancholica, fair as she is, has one fault in my eyes. It is that her beautiful lips have never yet curled into a smile, or that her exquisite eyes have never yet beamed with mirth. Were it permitted to me to move both with the laughter I feel persuaded lies hidden beneath that grave exterior, *she* would be perfect, and *I* would be happy!

KING.

Hear, hear! What do you say to *that*, daughter?

(PRINCESS *yawns : all her ladies yawn too.*)

KING.

What did you say?

PRINCESS.

I beg your pardon, I said nothing, papa. Am I expected to laugh at what the Prince said?

PRINCE ORPHEUS.

Oh, I've not begun yet; that was only a preliminary statement of my feelings, as it were!

PRINCESS.

Oh, I see! Do you really think, papa, it's any use his trying? (*yawns again.*)

KING.

It isn't a very hopeful beginning, I must say, for the young man. But you know the law! Every one, from king to beggar, who shall desire it, may take his chance. Prince Orpheus, begin! What can you do to make the Princess laugh?

PRINCE ORPHEUS.

Your Majesty, your Royal Highness, I will not say much, but I will put all my feelings into music! Perchance that may move the Princess to mirth. (*To an attendant*) Bring my ivory instrument.

KING (*curiously*).

What is it—a lyre ?

PRINCE ORPHEUS.

' No; I leave that to my grandfather. He is very fond of twanging it.

KING.

Let me guess. I like guessing ! Is it a piano ?

PRINCE ORPHEUS.

No, it isn't that either.

KING.

Perhaps it's the harp ?

PRINCE ORPHEUS.

No, it's more comic than that !

KING.

Then it's a banjo !

PRINCE ORPHEUS.

No. You are warmer, though.

KING.

Ha, ha! I've got it! The bones!

PRINCE ORPHEUS.

No, nor the bones either. Here it is—my silver-voiced, delicate lute, my ivory enchantress! (*takes a big comb from silver salver, which is brought to him by servant.*)

KING.

Ha, ha, ha! Very good! Very good indeed! Proceed. Now, daughter, have a care, or you will lose your cause yet!

PRINCE ORPHEUS.

I sincerely hope so! (*Blows on comb.*)

TUNE.—*I would I were a bird.*

KING (*laughing heartily*).

Ha, ha! Not bad! Not at all bad! Daughter, what say you?

PRINCESS (*drawing out her handkerchief*).

It moves me to tears with its loveliness! Oh, Prince, pray proceed!

PRINCE ORPHEUS (*doubtfully*).

Is the Princess laughing or crying, your Majesty?

KING (*vexed*).

Oh, she's piping her eye again. I never saw such a girl!

PRINCE ORPHEUS.

She must use a good many pocket-handkerchiefs in the course of a day, if she goes on at that rate!

SOBBINA.

Her Royal Highness, the Princess Melancholica, never uses less than fifty pocket-handkerchiefs a day.

PRINCESS (*drying her eyes*).

Pray go on, Prince! Let me hear another song! My very soul is unstrung with sweet grief!

KING.

Yes, have another try, my boy! And strike up a merry tune! I shall become melancholy myself if this goes on.

PRINCE ORPHEUS.

I'll do my best, sire.   (*Plays on comb the melody of* " *See, the conquering hero comes.*")

KING.

Ha, ha, ha !   This is excellent !   Well done, Prince ! You are a credit to your grandfather !   Daughter, beware, here comes *your* conquering hero !

PRINCESS (*coldly*).

Where, papa ?   *I* don't see him.

KING.

Why don't you laugh ?

PRINCESS.

Because I don't think it's funny.

KING.

Oh, dear ! oh, dear !   Prince, you have done very well.   It isn't your fault !   It's fate !   That's what it is—it's fate !   You may retire.   You have lost your cause.

PRINCE ORPHEUS (*sulkily*).

She'll never laugh if she won't laugh at that, it's my belief. (*Retires to background.*)

KING.

Next Prince forward! Prince Grimaldi!

> (PRINCE GRIMALDI *comes forward with a summer-sault, which lands him at the feet of the* PRINCESS.)

KING.

Ha, ha, ha! Capital! Oh, that is very good! Quite new, too! Prince, I congratulate you!

PRINCE GRIMALDI (*getting up eagerly, out of breath*).

Did she laugh at that, sire?

PRINCESS.

Laugh, indeed! I never saw such wretched fooling! Is there no circus in want of a clown?

PRINCE GRIMALDI.

I—oh—ah—what was your Royal Highness pleased to remark?

PRINCESS (*severely*).

Is there no circus in want of a clown, sir?

KING (*still laughing*).

Oh, dear! Is that all you can do, Prince?

PRINCE GRIMALDI.

Yes, sire, that's all. You see, I made quite sure that the Princess would laugh at *that!*

KING.

You must retire, I am afraid, Prince. It was a capital idea, but——

PRINCE GRIMALDI (*eagerly*).

Yes, I thought the idea was not bad——

KING.

By no means! Excellent! excellent! But you see the disheartening result. The Princess is no more to be moved to laughter than a signpost!—Next Prince, come up!

(PRINCE GRIMALDI *shrugs his shoulders, and retires to background.*)

PRINCESS.

Papa, dear, I *am* so tired!

KING.

Only one more, my pet—only one more! Then the ordeal is over for the week. Next Prince forward!

CHRISTY MINSTREL (*grinning and bowing*).

Me not a Prince—me a darkey!

KING.

Very well. All are alike here.

PRINCESS (*horrified*).

What a dreadful man! What eyes! What a shirt-collar! What gloves!

CHRISTY MINSTREL.

Do you like me—a pretty chicken? I thought so!

PRINCESS.

Sniffina, my salts, please! (SNIFFINA *hands them to her.*) Wait a minute, papa dear; I feel faint.

KING.

What's the matter now? Make haste, child!

PRINCESS (*sniffing prodigiously at smelling-bottle*).

Thank you, I feel better now!

KING (*to* MINSTREL).

Then you may begin.

CHRISTY MINSTREL.

Me sing a comic song, your Majesty. (*Rattles fantasia with banjo or bones, which he repeats at end of each verse.*)

TUNE.—*So early in the morning.*

De pretty girls in Darky land,
Dey always laugh and smile so bland,
Dey nebber sulk, dey nebber sigh,
Dey nebber pipe deir little eye ;
So early in de morning, so early in de morning,
So early in de morning, before de break of day.

Our pretty girls are smart and bright,
Dey laugh and show deir teeth so white,
Dey always chatter, talk and sing,
Dey giggle too like anyting,—
So early in de morning, so early in de morning,
So early in de morning, before de break of day.

PRINCESS (*sobbing*).

I *never*—NEVER—NEVER heard anything so melancholy in my life! Thank you so much!

KING.

Oh, confound it all! Will nothing ever make you laugh?

CHRISTY MINSTREL.

Good-bye! Me frightened! Me make ebbery one laugh,—and to-day me make de Princess cry! Me off! (*runs off.*)

KING.

Now, Melancholica, your suitors have departed for to-day, and it is nearly time for dinner. By the bye, there is one thing I always notice with satisfaction!

PRINCESS.

What may that be, my father?

KING.

It is this! No matter how mournful you are, you have always a very good appetite for your meals. Ha, ha!

U

PRINCESS (*very gravely*).

I cannot help that, papa, it's nature!

KING.

I don't say you can, my dear, I only say I observe it with extreme satisfaction, that is all! Before we go in to lunch, however, do me the favour, daughter, and look out on the great square and tell me what you see! (*Aside, rubbing his hands*) If she doesn't laugh at that, she'll never laugh at anything!

PRINCESS (*languidly*).

Is it another experiment of yours, papa dear, to make me laugh?

KING.

Please look out of the window, my dear!

PRINCESS.

No, but *is* it, papa?

KING.

Hem! Well—yes, it is!

PRINCESS.

Must I go ? You know it isn't any use at all ! And I'm *so* tired !

KING.

Don't say that, my dear, don't say that ! Do me the favour to look out of the window, that's all !

PRINCESS.

Well, to oblige you, I will; but really it is no use, papa, and you are always putting yourself to very unnecessary expense, I assure you ! (*Goes to side of stage and looks out of the window.*)

KING.

Well, daughter, what do you see ?

PRINCESS (*astonished*).

Why, the place is surely transformed, my father !

KING.

Just so ! Exactly ! Now, tell me what you see ?

PRINCESS.

Are the fountains spouting milk instead of water ?

KING.

Yes, my dear, and wine too !

PRINCESS.

Girls, come and look !   And all the trees are orna-
mented like Christmas-trees, with articles of clothing !

SOBBINA.

Oh, what lovely bonnets !

SNIFFINA.

And fans !

WIMPERINA.

And dresses !

KING.

Go on, go on !   What else ?

PRINCESS.

If my eyes do not deceive me, there are mountains
of cakes piled up !

SOBBINA.

Look at those boys eating away !

SNIFFINA.

And look at those old women at the milk-fountains!

WIMPERINA.

Oh, and the old men at the wine-fountains!

KING.

Well, child, what do you say to this? Look at those boys scrambling down below! Isn't it funny? Don't you laugh?

PRINCESS.

My father——

KING.

Well, my dear, does it tickle you—do you feel any inclination to laugh—eh?

PRINCESS.

My dearest father! *Laugh!!* Never has the idea been farther from my mind! Laugh indeed! What,— when your unbounded generosity provides for all the poor in the land! Unfeeling were the heart that could behold this scene and revel in heartless gaiety! Oh no, this demands my *tearful gratitude.* Look! I

thank you in tears, sire! I thank you in the name of
all the hungry and unclothed whom to-day you have
fed and attired! I thank you, papa dear, more than I
can say in words! Sobbina, another handkerchief!
(*Cries bitterly.*)

SOBBINA (*aside*).

There! I never!

SNIFFINA (*aside*).

It's no use!

WIMPERINA (*aside*).

I must say it's rather hard on the poor King!

KING.

Oh, confound it! She's thanking me in tears! As
if I wanted that! It's too bad, I declare! Speak,
Melancholica! Will nothing *ever* make you laugh?

PRINCESS (*sadly, but firmly*).

No, papa! NEVER!

Enter SERVANT.

SERVANT.

If you please, your Majesty, there's a peculiar young man outside, with a funny set of people, and he says he wants to see you.

KING.

Oh, bother it—I'm vexed—I don't wish to see any one! Stay—never mind, it's all the same, I suppose, whether I see him or don't see him. Tell him he may come in !

SERVANT.

So, please your Majesty, here he is, and all his company. (*Aside*) Circus people, I suppose!

[*Exit.*

Enter JACK *leading the* SWAN, *to which are still attached* POLLY, *the* SWEEP, *the* POLICEMAN, *the* BURGOMASTER, *the* BURGOMASTER'S WIFE, *and the* CLOWN.

KING.

Hullo ! what's all this ?

PRINCESS (*starts and stares with all her might, then suddenly bursts out laughing*).

Ha, ha, ha!—Ha, ha, ha, ha, ha!—Ha, ha, ha, ha, ha!—Ha, ha, ha, ha, ha!—Ha, ha, ha!—Ha, ha, ha!—Ha, ha!——

KING.

What do I hear?

PRINCESS.

Ha, ha, ha!—Ha, ha, ha!—Ha, ha, ha, ha, ha!—Ha, ha, ha!

SOBBINA
SNIFFINA
WIMPERINA
} (*giggling*). He, he, he!—He, he, he! He, he, he, he!——

KING.

My daughter laughing!—Ho, ho, ho!

PRINCESS.

Ha, ha, ha, ha!—Ha, ha, ha! Oh, I can't laugh any more! My side does ache so! I'm not accustomed to laughing! Ha, ha, ha!——

JACK (*bowing to* PRINCESS).

Are *you* the Princess who never laughs?

PRINCESS.

Yes, I am!   Ha, ha, ha!—Ha, ha, ha!

KING.

Ho, ho!   She is the Princess Melancholica, she is!

PRINCESS.

Ha, ha, ha, ha, ha!

JACK.

So I see.

POLLY.

Oh, please, your Royal Highness, to command this young man to release me!

PRINCESS.

Ha, ha, ha!

SWEEP.

If your Majesty will set me free, I will sweep all your Majesty's royal chimneys for nothing!

PRINCESS.

Ha, ha, ha!   Ladies, please hold me, I am going to pieces with laughing, I think!   Ha, ha, ha!

LADIES.

It is very funny!   He, he, he!

KING.

Young man, whoever you may be, welcome as my son-in-law, for you are the first who has made her laugh!   Ho, ho!

JACK.

If the Princess will have me, I am sure I shall not object!

PRINCESS.

I will marry you if you promise always to make me laugh.   I like laughing!—Ha, ha, ha!

LADIES.

He, he, he!

KING.

Ho, ho, ho!—This is splendid!   I shall go out of my skin with joy!

JACK.

I will do my best.

BURGOMASTER.

Oh, please let me go now!

WIFE.

And me too!

CLOWN.

Include me, your Majesty!

POLICEMAN.

And me as well!

PRINCESS.

Ha, ha, ha!

JACK (*touching* CLOWN).

Off you go!

CLOWN (*running off*).

You wait till I get my hot poker, Mr. Jack!

[*Exit.*

PRINCESS.

Ha, ha, ha!

JACK (*touching* BURGOMASTER'S WIFE).

You go next!

WIFE (*running off*).

Wait till I get a chance to pay you out, young man !

[*Exit.*

PRINCESS.

Ha, ha, ha !

JACK (*touching* BURGOMASTER).

Follow your wife !

BURGOMASTER (*going off*).

Small thanks to you !   Policeman, see if I don't pay you out for getting me into this scrape !   [*Exit.*

PRINCESS.

Ha, ha, ha !

JACK (*touching* POLICEMAN).

Move on, old fellow !

POLICEMAN (*running off*).

If he means to get me into trouble, I think I'll run in another direction !   [*Exit.*

PRINCESS.

Ha, ha, ha !

JACK (*touching* SWEEP).

Now, Smutty, it's your turn !

SWEEP (*running off*).

Catch me ever trying to help a young woman again, that's all !   [*Exit.*

PRINCESS.

Ha, ha, ha !

JACK (*touching* POLLY).

Last, but not least, I set you free, apologizing humbly for having caused you any inconvenience !

POLLY (*running off*).

Shouldn't I just like to scratch your eyes out, my fine young fellow !   [*Exit.*

JACK.

Always supposing I allowed you to do it !

PRINCESS.

Ha, ha, ha !

LADIES.

He, he, he !

KING.

Ho, ho, ho !. My dear fellow, I never saw such capital fun in my life ! But tell me, how came those people to be so very foolish as to get stuck to that bird ?

JACK.

May it please your Majesty to stroke it ?

KING.

With pleasure. (*Strokes* SWAN.) Pretty Swan ! nice Swan ! (SWAN *screams loudly.*)

JACK.

" Swan, Swan,
Hold on ! "

KING.

What's this ? Help me, daughter !

PRINCESS.

Ha, ha, ha ! Pa, you're stuck fast ! (*Helps to pull off* KING. SWAN *screams.*)

JACK.

" Swan, Swan,
Hold on !"

There, now *you* are tight and fast! And now you
are both in my power, I ask you once again, your
Majesty, will you give me the Princess for wife ?

KING.

With the greatest pleasure in life !

JACK.

Princess, will you marry me ?

PRINCESS.

Certainly I will.   I like you !

JACK (*touching both*).

You are free !   But—mind and keep your word !

SWAN (*loudly calling*).

" Come, come, come !
My work is done
Ere set of sun,
The Princess won,
Come, come, come !"

Enter DAME TROT.

DAME TROT.

So, Jack, the stupid bird has made your fortune after all, I see!

JACK (*abashed*).

I have to thank you for it!

DAME TROT.

Now you want him no longer, I shall take him again. Now the Princess has laughed, the spell is broken, and she shall be called Melancholica no longer, but the Princess Ha-ha! Live happily, and in your happiness sometimes think of me! Don't you think now, Jack, a *Pig* or a *Goose* would have been more useful?

JACK (*bursting out laughing*).

Ha, ha, ha!

PRINCESS		Ha, ha, ha, ha!
KING		Ho, ho, ho!
SOBBINA	(*all together*).	He, he, he!
SNIFFINA		He, he!
WIMPERINA		He!

CURTAIN.

DE PRETTY GIRLS.

1. De pret-ty girls in Darkey land, Dey always laugh and smile so bland, Dey
2. Our pretty girls are smart and bright, Dey laugh and shew deir teeth so white, Dey

neb-ber sulk, dey neb-ber sigh, Dey neb-ber pipe deir lit - tle eye, So
al-ways chatter, talk, and sing, Dey gig-gle too like a - ny-ting, So

ear - ly in de morning, So ear - ly in de morning, So

ear - ly in de morn-ing, Be - fore de break of day.

www.ingramcontent.com/pod-product-compliance
Lightning Source LLC
Chambersburg PA
CBHW031337070726
47496CB00017B/1178